"I think that you're starting to like it here," Vic said.

She swallowed as their eyes held.

"I am. It's peaceful," she said finally, fully aware of the calloused warmth of his hand.

"It can be," he said. "Winter can be harsh and wild, though. When the wind whips up snow and piles it into snowbanks, blocks off roads."

"I've never been here in the winter, except when I was a little girl," she said.

"It has its own beauty," Vic continued. "Its own moments when the sun comes out and the world looks like an endless blanket of white."

His voice and the pictures he sketched with it were beguiling, and Lauren imagined herself tucked away in her father's ranch house, looking out over blinding fields of white, a fire blazing in the hearth, a book on her lap.

It's a dream, her practical self told her. A foolish dream.

She tugged her hand free and pulled herself away from Vic and the web he was weaving.

Carolyne Aarsen and her husband, Richard, live on a small ranch in northern Alberta, where they have raised four children and numerous foster children and are still raising cattle. Carolyne crafts her stories in an office with a large west-facing window, through which she can watch the changing seasons while struggling to make her words obey. Visit her website at carolyneaarsen.com.

Visit the Author Profile page at Harlequin.com for more titles.

Trusting the Cowboy

Carolyne Aarsen

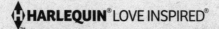

Recycling programs
for this product may
not exist in your area.

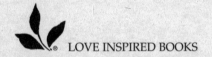

LOVE INSPIRED BOOKS

ISBN-13: 978-0-373-81918-8

Trusting the Cowboy

www.Harlequin.com

Printed in U.S.A.

Trust in the Lord with all your heart
and lean not on your own understanding;
in all your ways submit to Him,
and He will make your paths straight.
—*Proverbs* 3:5–6

To my husband, Richard,
who has shown me the meaning of trust.

Chapter One

She wasn't supposed to be here yet. Her sister Jodie had told him she was arriving in a couple of weeks.

But there she sat, perched in one of Drake's worn chairs, as out of place in the shabby lawyer's office as a purebred filly in a petting zoo.

Lauren McCauley appeared to be every inch the businesswoman Vic knew her to be. Tall. Slim. Blond hair twisted up in some fancy bun, a few wisps falling around her delicate features. She wore a brown blazer over a fitted dress tucked under her legs. Her high heels made her look as if she might topple to the ground if she stood.

A silver laptop rested on her knees and she frowned at the screen.

When she was a teenager, coming to Montana to visit her dad during the summer, she'd had a look that promised great beauty. But she always managed to seem cool and unapproachable. And she had never been his type.

Vic leaned more toward girls who rode horses and weren't afraid to get their hands dirty mucking out horse stalls, running a tractor or feeding cows.

In spite of that, Vic couldn't help a faint flutter of attraction when he peeked over at her again. She'd always been pretty. Now she looked stunning.

Lauren McCauley glanced up from the laptop she was typing on with her manicured fingers. She gave him a polite smile, her lips glistening a pale peach color, and she turned back to the computer.

Dissed and dismissed, he thought, glancing down at his cleanest blue jeans with the faded knees and the twill shirt he'd figured would be good enough. Now it seemed scruffy with its worn cuffs and grease stain on the arm. He felt exactly like the cowboy he was.

He pulled his hat off his head and walked over to where Jane Forsythe, Drake's secretary, pounded on her keyboard, glowering through her cat's-eye glasses at the computer screen. The overhead light burnished the copper of her hair, making it look even brassier than the fake color everyone knew it to be.

"Hey, Vic, you handsome cowboy, you." Jane tugged off her reading glasses and tossed them on a pile of papers that threatened to topple. "Drake will be right with you." She angled her head to look past him to where Lauren sat, then leaned forward, her hand cupping her mouth. "He has to see *her* first." Jane put emphasis on the *her* as if Lauren were some strange species of woman.

"That's fine. I'm early," Vic said. "But let him know I'm here." He took a chair along the other wall. There were two empty ones on either side of Lauren, but he felt more comfortable giving himself some distance.

Besides, he had a better view of Lauren from this angle.

"Always so responsible," Jane said approvingly, slipping her glasses on. "How's your mother?"

"She has her days. It's been hard."

"Losing a parent can be difficult," Jane said. She looked past him again at Lauren. Vic guessed from the way the secretary scrunched up her face in sympathy, she was getting ready to take a stab at distracting Lauren from her work. "And how are you doing, Miss McCauley? It's only been a few months since your own father died. Vic here lost his father, too, about four months ago. You two could compare notes."

Vic forced himself not to roll his eyes. Jane had a good heart and meant well, but for the secretary of a lawyer she was completely unaware of personal privacy and space.

Lauren's gaze rested on Jane, then shifted to Vic, her eyes a soft gray blue fringed with thick lashes.

"You're Vic Moore, aren't you?"

"Yes, I am," he said. "I rent your father's ranch."

"I thought Rusty Granger did."

"Not for the past three years."

Vic wasn't surprised Lauren didn't know that. After her parents' divorce, when Lauren was about nine, she and her sisters had lived for ten months of the year with their grandmother in Knoxville. Two years later, after their mother died, they came to the ranch for the summer to visit their father. But when Lauren turned eighteen, she and her twin sister, Erin, stopped coming. The last time he remembered seeing Lauren here was maybe four years ago, and then only for a few days.

Their younger sister, Jodie, ducked out of her last visit when she was seventeen and never came back at all. She had returned a couple of months ago, to fulfill the terms of their father's will, and was now living here permanently.

Everything he knew about Lauren, Vic had learned over time while working with Keith McCauley on his ranch as well as the occasional coffee-shop chitchat at the Grill and Chill, Saddlebank's local restaurant. Though chitchat was the wrong thing to call the steady litany of complaints Keith leveled at anyone who would listen about life, the government, the lax sheriff's department and his wayward daughters.

The rest he'd learned recently from Lauren's sister Jodie, now engaged to Vic's good friend Finn Hicks. He knew Lauren worked as an accountant. That she was single and dedicated to her career.

Still not his type.

"I shouldn't be surprised Rusty isn't renting it anymore," Lauren said, giving him a polite smile and closing her laptop. Either she had finished whatever it was she was working on or she had given up. "My father never particularly cared for him."

Vic held his tongue. Keith hadn't cared for too many people, so Vic had handled the man carefully. Vic and Keith had had a lease-to-own agreement for Vic to buy Keith's ranch.

Vic wanted to ask Lauren more about her plans. He knew that she was here to satisfy the terms of her father's will, as well. Her sister Jodie, who was coming to the end of her obligation, had told him all about the conditions their father had put on the girls inheriting the ranch.

Two of the three girls had to stay at the ranch for two months each before all three of them could make a final decision.

He'd spoken to Jodie about his deal with her father. But all she could tell him was that she'd have to defer to Lauren's wishes, and all she knew was that Lauren was agreeable to selling.

But he wasn't about to bring that up now. He still had a couple of months.

"I heard you'll be staying at your father's place while you're here," he said. "Jodie was excited to see you."

"Yes. Jodie said she got my old room ready. I'm headed there next."

"Is Erin coming back?"

Lauren shook her head. "If I stay the two months, she won't have to, and Jodie and I will make the final decision on what to do with the ranch."

She didn't seem to know anything about the deal he'd made with her father, either.

Her cell phone rang and she pulled it out of her purse.

She turned away from him, speaking in a low voice, and he tried not to listen. However, in the small room, it was hard not to. The man on the other end had a loud voice and Vic heard snatches of conversation.

"I'm at the lawyer's office…I can't make a final decision until I speak to him… Of course I'm leaving after my time is done. I've no intention of sticking around." She pressed her lips together and fingered a strand of hair away from her face. "Your offer is fantastic, but I need to talk to my sisters first, but yes, I think you'll get it."

A chill slid through his veins.

Was she talking about the ranch?

He swallowed down a knot as she spoke again.

"Come down in a week or so and I can show you the ranch. That's all I can say for now…fine…see you then." She ended the call, a frown creasing the perfection of her forehead. Then she dropped the phone in her purse.

The room felt short of air as the reality of what she was talking about sank in.

"Was that a buyer for the ranch?" he blurted out before he could stop himself.

Her look of surprise clearly showed him what she thought of what he had just done. But it didn't matter. It was out there now.

"Actually, yes. It was."

"But I had a purchase deal with your father," he said, trying to keep the frustration out of his voice. "That's why I was renting it."

She lifted her chin, her hands folded primly on her laptop. "Jodie mentioned your situation to me, but we could find no paperwork substantiating your claim."

"Your father told me he'd taken care of it." Vic remembered discussing this with Keith after his cancer diagnosis, knowing that they needed to get something in writing to protect their agreement. Keith had promised him he was putting his affairs in order. That he'd written something out for him and signed it.

"As I said, we didn't find anything. But if you're interested in purchasing the ranch, you'll have an opportunity to counteroffer."

Vic stared at her, doubts dogging him. Keith had given him a deal on the price and Vic knew it. He doubted Lauren would do the same for the future buyer or for him.

Fury at Keith's failure to keep his promise surged through him.

The intercom beeped. Jane answered it, then she looked at Lauren.

"Drake will see you now," she said, her eyes darting from Lauren to Vic and back again.

Vic pressed his lips together as Lauren slipped her laptop in her leather briefcase, picked it up and stood all in one smooth motion.

But as she took a step, her purse strap caught on the chair. She stumbled and Vic jumped up to help her, catching her by the elbow, which made her totter. Her briefcase fell. She jerked her arm away. "I'm okay. I don't need your help."

He didn't say anything but bent down to pick up her briefcase. But she moved too quickly and snatched it off the floor.

She spared him a glance as she straightened. Then she strode across the carpet in her towering heels, shoulders straight, head high.

And as the door closed behind her, Vic slumped back in his chair, dragging his hand over his face, feeling stupid and scared.

He'd just about made a fool of himself in front of this woman.

Lauren had a buyer for the ranch.

And there was no paper from her father.

He had promised his younger brother,

Dean, that they were getting the ranch. Guaranteed it. Now they might lose it.

If that happened, how was he supposed to help his brother?

"Lauren, how lovely to see you," Drake Neubauer said, getting up from behind his desk.

Outwardly Lauren was smiling but her insides still shook and her hands still trembled.

Mr. Vic Moore had looked so angry when she told him about the buyer for the ranch.

You did nothing wrong, she told herself, taking a deep breath as Drake walked toward her outstretched hand. *He has no claim.*

You could have let him help you.

She dismissed that voice as quickly as it slid into her brain. She'd been doing fine until he'd interfered and almost made her fall.

And wouldn't that have come across all dignified?

"So glad you could make it here," Drake said as he shook her hand, his other hand covering it, squeezing lightly. "Goodness, girl, your hands are like ice."

"I'm just cold-blooded," she joked as she returned his warm handshake.

Harvey had always accused her of that. At

least that was the excuse he gave her when he dumped her a few days before their wedding.

"It's good to be back," she said, relegating those shameful memories to where they belonged. The past.

"I'm sure you missed all this," Drake said, waving one hand at the window behind them.

Drake's offices were situated above the hardware store, and through the window Lauren saw the valley the Saddlebank River snaked through. Her eyes shifted to the mountains, snow frosted and craggy, cradling the basin, and her mind slowed. Though she and her sisters had resented coming here every summer, when they were back home in Knoxville she'd found herself missing these very mountains.

"It was a part of my life," she said, her voice quiet.

"Does it feel good to be back?" Drake asked.

Lauren gave him a brief smile as she lowered herself to the chair, setting her briefcase on the floor and tucking her skirt under her legs. "Yes, it does." Though the restless part of her wasn't sure how she would stay busy on the ranch, the weary part longed for a reprieve from the stress and tension of the last year and a half.

And a break from the pitying stares of

friends each time they met. Harvey hadn't only taken a wedding away from her, he'd also robbed her of her money, her dignity and her self-esteem. She had been scrambling to show to the world that he hadn't won.

"And how are you doing since your father's passing? Ironic that it wasn't the cancer that killed him but a truck accident." Drake sat down, opened the file lying on his desk and flipped through it.

She wasn't sure how to respond, so she said nothing.

Though losing her father had bothered her more than she'd thought it would, the true reality was neither Lauren nor her sisters had ever been close with Keith McCauley.

"Has the accident been cleared with the insurance company yet?" Lauren asked as Drake made a few notes on a piece of paper in the file. "Jodie had said there were some difficulties?"

"They're still dealing with it, but last I heard, it should be finalized in the next few weeks."

"Where is the truck?"

"At Vic Moore's. The accident happened as your father was going down his driveway."

"Any liability at play?"

"No. That much has been determined already. The truck was in perfect working order."

"And Vic's driveway?"

"Your father hit a deer, then lost control and rolled the vehicle. Neither Vic nor the Rocking M were at fault."

"I wasn't thinking of filing a lawsuit, if that's what you were worried about," Lauren said, her mind ticking back to the tall man still sitting in the waiting room. With his dark eyebrows, firm chin and square jaw, he commanded attention. When he had stridden into the office, she had been unable to look away.

But all it took was a glance at her bare ring finger and her father's will to remind her of the hard lessons life had taught her about men. Men were selfish and undependable. Between her father, Harvey and her now-former boss, she should be crystal clear on that point.

In Christ alone...

The words of a song she had been singing lately slipped into her mind, and she latched on to them. Men might not be able to give anything up for loved ones, but Christ had.

Which only reminded her again that she needed to be self-sufficient and self-reliant.

"No. Of course not." But Drake's hasty answer, and the way he fluttered one hand in a defensive gesture, told her that he had, indeed, thought exactly that.

She tried not to feel overly sensitive, reminding herself that Drake knew nothing about her other than what her father had told him.

"So I'm guessing you're here to officially check in," Drake said, settling into his chair behind his desk.

"Or clock in," Lauren returned. "I wasn't sure of the protocol, and I did end up coming a couple of weeks earlier than anticipated." Getting laid off was a stark motivator.

"No. It's fine." Drake gave her an apologetic smile. "I know your father had his reasons for doing this, and just for the record, I tried to talk him out of it. Tried to explain to him that it could come across as being manipulative."

Lauren shrugged. "Let's be honest here. Like Jodie said after the funeral, it seemed he never gave us anything without strings attached."

Her words came out more bitter than she'd intended. Though she and her father hadn't had the adversarial relationship he and Jodie had, they hadn't been close, either.

"I'm sorry, but at least not all three of you

had to stay here. You can decide what to do after your two months are up."

Lauren heard the unspoken question in his voice and decided to address it directly.

"Erin said she would go along with whatever decision I make, but you may as well know that we will be selling the ranch."

"To Vic?"

Lauren shook her head. "No. I have a buyer lined up. A client from the firm I worked… used to work for. He has various real estate holdings and has been looking for another investment opportunity. When I told him about the ranch, he was interested."

"But Vic has rented your father's land for the past three years. I thought they had an agreement."

"Is that going to be a problem?" Lauren straightened, leaning forward, her heart racing at the thought that he might jeopardize the sale. She would receive one-third of the proceeds, and she would need every penny of that for her new business venture. A venture that she was in a rush to put together after losing her current job. "Does he have a legal right to the property?"

"As far as I know, your father never gave me anything in writing, if that's what you're concerned about. I believe it was a handshake deal. Not uncommon around here."

"So I have no legal obligation to sell it to Mr. Moore?"

"None whatsoever. But I do have to warn you, your father was thinking of drawing up something legal for Vic. If that is the case, and this paper does show up, it will need to be dealt with."

"Had he mentioned a price?"

Drake gave her a number.

It wasn't close to what her potential buyer was offering. "And if such documentation isn't found?"

"Then he has no claim."

Relief flooded her. "That's good to know. I don't want anything preventing the sale." Or forcing her to sell it to Vic at a significantly reduced price.

As far as she knew, Jodie hadn't found any paperwork, so it seemed they were in the clear.

"A word of advice, if I may, Lauren," Drake continued. "You might want to give him a chance to counteroffer or at least match what your buyer is willing to pay."

"Of course. I could do that."

"I know he was hoping to get the ranch for his younger brother, Dean."

Lauren dredged her memory and came up with a picture of a young man who partied hard and spent the rest of the time riding rodeo. And trying to date her twin sister, Erin. "Dean is ranching now?"

"Not at the moment. He was injured in a rodeo accident a while back. Vic leased your father's ranch with an eye to adding it to his holdings and making room for Dean."

"Tell Vic to talk to me if he wants to make an offer. He's waiting to see you next."

"Why don't you tell him yourself?"

Lauren thought back to the anger he'd revealed when she told him she had a buyer, then shook her head. "No. Better if it comes from a third party."

"Okay. I'll tell him to come up with some numbers." Drake tapped his pen on the open file in front of him. "Is there anything else I can help you with?"

"Not right now. Like I said, I wanted to check in."

Drake leaned back in his chair, looking as if he had a few more things he wanted to discuss, then he shook his head and stood up. "Okay. You know how to get in touch with me if you have any further questions."

She got up and Drake came around the desk to escort her to the door. But before he opened it, his eyes caught hers, his expression serious. "Again, I'm so sorry about your father. I wish you girls had had a chance to get some closure in your relationship before he died."

"Jodie mentioned some letters that Dad wrote to each of us before he died. Maybe that will help."

"He was a sad and lonely man," Drake said.

Lauren forced back her initial response and the guilt that always nipped at her. "I know we should have come to visit more often," she agreed. And that was all she was going to say. The burden of guilt shouldn't lie so heavy on her shoulders. Her father could have initiated some contact, as well.

She thanked Drake again and walked through the door.

Vic still sat there, but as she came out, he stood, his hat in his hand, his eyes on her. The gesture seemed so courtly, and for some reason it touched her.

"I need to talk to you" was all he said, his words clipped.

Lauren did not want to deal with this right now.

"I'm going to presume it has to do with your agreement with my father," she said, weariness tingeing her voice, dragging at her limbs. She felt as if she'd been fighting this exhaustion for the past year. The stress of losing her job and trying to start a new business, and now needing to fulfill the terms of her father's will, had made every decision seem momentous. Impossible.

"Can we talk now? Can I buy you a coffee at the Grill and Chill?"

"Not really. I just want to get to the ranch."

"Meeting at the ranch would work better. We could do this right away."

This was certainly not the homecoming she had expected, but in spite of her fatigue she sensed he wouldn't let go. "May as well get this over and done with," she said.

"I'll meet you there in an hour."

Lauren nodded, then walked to the door, disconcerted when he pulled it open for her, standing aside to let her through.

"Thank you," she murmured, thankful she had worn her heels to see Drake Neubauer.

Though she doubted they'd made an impression on the lawyer, as she glanced up at Vic she appreciated the advantage they gave her.

The grim set of Vic's jaw and his snapping brown eyes below dark, slashing brows sent a shiver down her spine that told her he would be trouble.

Chapter Two

Vic parked his truck beside Lauren's car and gave himself a moment to catch his breath, center himself. He rested his hands on the steering wheel and looked out over the Rocking M. The house stood on a rise of land overlooking the corrals below. The corrals and pasture eased toward the Saddlebank River on one side and the rolling hills leading to the mountains on the other. So often he had driven this yard, imagining his brother living here

It was the promise he'd held out to Dean and himself that got him through the past ten months.

A way to assuage his own guilt over the fact that he had been too late to get Dean off that rank bronc at the rodeo. As a pickup man, it was Vic's job to get the riders safely off the horse as soon as he saw they were in trouble.

But Vic had had other things on his mind that day. Other things that drew his attention.

It had only been a few seconds, the smallest moment when Vic made eye contact with Dean's ex-girlfriend Tiffany sitting in the arena a few feet away. Smiling at her. Thinking about how they could be together again. She had told him that she'd broken up with Dean. She had called out to him just before Dean's ride and blown him a kiss.

Then Vic had turned his head in time to catch the sight branded into his brain forever.

The bronc Dean was riding spinning away from where he and his horse were, ready. The horse making another turn, crushing Dean's leg against the temporary panels set up in the arena. Dean's leg getting caught in the crossbars as the horse pulled away.

Vic still heard his brother's cries of agony, saw him writhing on the ground in the arena.

The girlfriend walked away from both of them a week later. Dean started walking four months later.

His brother still struggled with resentment and anger over what had happened.

And Vic wrestled with a guilt that gnawed at him each time he saw his brother grimace in pain. Each time he listened to Dean talk about how Tiffany had broken his heart.

Buying Keith McCauley's ranch was supposed to fix all that.

And now?

Please, Lord, let that piece of paper be somewhere in the house. I need this place for Dean.

The prayer surged upward as he eased out of the truck, heading up the walk, the futility of it clawing at him. He and Jodie had discussed it only briefly, but she hadn't found any evidence of this agreement.

Maybe she hadn't searched hard enough, he thought as he trudged up the stairs to the house. Maybe his presence would coax it out of its hiding place.

Keith hadn't left anything about the lease agreement at Drake's and he hadn't given anything to Vic, so the only other place it could be was here. In Keith's office in the ranch house.

As he sent up another prayer, he knocked on the door.

He heard laughter from within, and he eased out a wry smile. His own house was a somber, sad place. His father's death a few months ago had only added to the heavy atmosphere looming over the house since Dean came home from the hospital three months before that, disabled and bitter. There'd been no laughter in the Moore household for a long time.

No one came to the door, so he rang the doorbell. Cheerful chimes pealed through the house, then he heard footsteps coming.

He wasn't surprised to see Jodie answer, her head tipped to one side, her dark hair caught back in a loose ponytail, her bangs skimming eyes so blue they looked unnatural.

They were a different blue than Lauren's, which were more gray. Cooler.

He shook that thought off. Lauren was attractive, yes, but he had to keep a level head. Too much was at stake to be distracted by a good-looking woman.

"Hey, Vic. Lauren said you were coming," Jodie said, stepping aside to let him in. "I thought you'd be here sooner."

"I had to stop at the dealership to get some parts for my horse trailer." Nestor, who owned the place, had been particularly chatty. Then John Argall stopped in and asked him how Dean was doing and if Vic was coming back to Bible study. Vic had felt bad at the disappointment John had displayed. The past month he had taken on extra work. Work Dean would have done.

He didn't blame his brother. Dean wasn't as sure as Vic was that Keith had made proper arrangements to protect their handshake agreement so he went back to work for Jan Peter, a local carpenter. Vic hadn't signed anything, but Keith had assured him that he had written something up.

He just needed to find it. Then Dean could stop working for Jan and they could start ranching together.

"Come in," Jodie was saying. "Lauren and I were catching up. She's trying to talk me out of purple bridesmaid dresses."

"You're not looking for my opinion, I hope?"

"I thought you could weigh in. When Lauren has an idea, she's immovable."

That didn't bode well for any negotiations, Vic thought.

"Can't say I have a lot of expertise in that area. I'm only standing up for Finn, and he told me to wear clean blue jeans."

"Listen, mister, when it comes to wedding attire, you check with me before you check with my future husband." But she spoke in a cheerful tone, adding a wink.

He returned Jodie's smile, wide and open and happy, a much different woman than the one who'd come to Saddlebank with a chip on her shoulder and a cocky attitude. Now, engaged to Vic's good friend Finn Hicks, she looked relaxed. Happy.

Vic wondered what Jodie thought of the potential buyer of the ranch and if she liked the idea. He was thinking of asking her but quashed that thought as he toed off his boots. He had to figure this out on his own. Bringing Jodie in would only create complications.

He set his scuffed and cracked cowboy boots beside Lauren's high heels, the contrast making him laugh.

"We're sitting in the dining room. Do you want some coffee?"

"Sure. Sounds good." He followed Jodie through the kitchen. His steps slowed as he passed Keith's office, which was opposite the eating bar of the kitchen, and he glanced inside the open door.

Papers covered the desk that ran along one wall. The filing cabinet's top drawer was open.

"We've been going through Dad's stuff," Jodie said, catching the direction of his gaze. "I meant to do it when I first came but thought I would wait till Lauren was here. She's the organized one."

He suppressed the question that nagged at him. He had time yet. Lauren might have a buyer all lined up, but she still had to stay at the ranch for two months before she could make a decision.

He followed Jodie to the end of the house. Vaulted ceilings soaring two stories high arched over the living and dining room. Light from the upper windows slanted down into the space. A fireplace made of river rock bisected the far wall, framed by large bay windows overlooking the pasture and the mountains.

To his left a set of stairs led to the loft and a couple of bedrooms above, and the basement with its bedrooms downstairs. He knew the layout of the house because he had spent time here before.

Though all those stairs might not be best for Dean at the moment, his leg would get better. Vic had to believe that. And when he did, it would be a perfect place for his brother to live. A real home.

"Sit down. Ignore the mess," Jodie said as she padded barefoot to the kitchen. She wore blue jeans, frayed at the cuffs, and a gauzy purple and pink shirt that had tiny bells sewn to the hem. The bells created a happy tinkling sound as she took a mug out of the cupboard and poured him some coffee.

Lauren, in her stark dress and hair still

pulled back in a bun, was a complete contrast to her sister. She glanced up from papers strewn over the table. Her dark-framed glasses gave her an austere air. She held his eyes for a moment, then looked away.

Dismissed once again, he thought, remembering their earlier encounter too well.

"Finn told me you're working the rodeo coming up?" Jodie said, setting the mug of coffee on the table.

"Yeah. Walden was short a pickup man, so I thought I'd help out." Vic settled in the chair across from Lauren, taking the cup with a smile of thanks.

"You always were a pickup artist," Jodie joked as she sat as well and shuffled through the papers in front of her.

"Oldest joke in the book," Vic groaned.

"I feel like I should know what a pickup man is," Lauren said, slipping her glasses off her face and setting them on the table.

"See that, Vic?" Jodie said, her voice holding a note of admiration. "That's why I should wear glasses. People think you're all smart and important. And when you take them off, it looks like you're getting ready to do business. People take glasses-wearing people seriously."

Vic chuckled as Lauren shot her sister a

wry look. "You should take that show on the road," Lauren said.

"It's my only joke," Jodie said with a grin. "Wouldn't take me far."

"Oh, I'm sure you have more you could add to your repertoire," Lauren said, smiling back at her sister.

"You'd have to come with me as my straight man, though. A role you play to perfection."

Lauren laughed again and Vic couldn't look away. She was a beautiful woman in her own right. But now, relaxed, smiling, a glint of humor in her eyes as she teased her sister, the light from the window behind her lighting her hair, she was luminous.

He groaned inwardly as he took a sip of his coffee, frustrated with his response to this woman. He was here to talk business and he was coming up with mental compliments?

"Getting back to my original question, what is a pickup man?" Lauren asked.

Vic waited for Jodie to answer, but she was frowning at a piece of paper, seemingly unaware of her sister's question. So Vic replied.

"We ride along the outskirts of the arena during the rough stock events—bareback, saddle bronc, bull and steer riding. We help the guys off the horses if we can, make sure the bulls and horses get out of the arena safely. That kind of thing."

"I see," said Lauren, the vague tone of her voice conveying her lack of interest.

"I know Walden is glad you'll be there," Jodie said. "He told me you guys work well together."

"Who's Walden?" Lauren asked.

"The other pickup man," Vic said. "We always work in pairs."

"You'll have to come to the rodeo, Lauren. See Vic in action," Jodie said. "And that horse that Finn trained. Adelaide, one of his clients, will be riding it in the barrel riding competition."

"We'll see how that works out." Lauren's polite smile seemed to dismiss that line of conversation. She slipped her glasses on her face and it was back to business. "We've been looking through our father's papers and so far haven't found anything referring to your deal."

Vic glanced down at the folders lying on the table between them, resisting the impulse to riffle through them himself. "Your father and I agreed on a lease-to-buy agreement," Vic said, struggling to keep his tone even. Pragmatic. "Are you sure he didn't say anything about that to you or make a note of it anywhere?"

Lauren shook her head, picking up another file and opening it. "We haven't seen everything yet, mind you, but it doesn't look good."

"Are there any files left? Did he have anything on the computer?"

Lauren frowned as she held his gaze. "Dad didn't do much on the computer," she said, dismissing that possibility. "Besides, we couldn't figure out the password on it. I don't suppose you would know?"

"Not a clue. Did you try the horses' names?"

"Yeah. And his birth date, our birth dates—though I doubt he remembered them anyway—and in a pinch his and Mom's anniversary. The name of the ranch. Nothing."

"I can't help you there." He didn't know Keith that well.

"Even if we could log on, I doubt there's anything there, and even there was documentation, if it wasn't signed…" Her voice trailed off.

Annoyance snaked through him. It was so easy for her to dismiss his claim. She didn't know what was at stake.

"Would you mind if I looked through the papers myself?"

Her lips tightened and he wondered if she

was afraid he might find something that would help his case. He held her eyes, as if challenging her, then she looked at Jodie.

"What do you think?" she asked her sister.

"I don't care," Jodie said with a shrug. "If Vic has a claim, maybe we need to see if we can find evidence for it. He might know better what he's looking for."

Lauren nodded and turned back to Vic, taking her glasses off again, ignoring Jodie's chuckle at her action. "I doubt you'd find what you want. But if we don't discover anything, I'm willing to sell the ranch to you, provided you can match the buyer's price."

"What price is that?"

When she named it, Vic's mouth fell open as blood surged to his throat and chest, threatening to choke off his breathing.

There was no way he could meet that amount, but there was also no way he was telling her that. He swallowed hard and tried to claim some remnants of composure.

"I'll have to talk my banker," he said, attempting to inject some confidence into his voice. "But before I do that, I'd like to make sure that there is absolutely no evidence of the agreement. And I'd like to look for myself."

Lauren gave him a tight nod. "I guess that's fair, though, like I said, we didn't find anything. You'd have to come here, though. To look at the papers. And one of us will have to be here."

"You don't trust me?" The words burst out of him before he could stop them.

Way to create a good impression.

Jodie patted him on the shoulder. "We trust you, Vic." She turned to Lauren. "I trust him. He's Finn's friend and a good guy."

"Don't take it personally," Lauren said, her mouth twisting in a cool smile. "I don't trust any man." Then she turned to Jodie. "But as far as his agreement with our father is concerned, there are other factors at play. If he finds something that corroborates his claim, it's best that it happens here with us watching. That way no one can challenge it."

He. His. She spoke of him as if he suddenly wasn't there.

Vic took another sip of his coffee, reminding himself that he just had to get through this.

And, more than ever, he had to find some evidence of the deal he and Keith had drawn up.

There was no other choice.

"Confess. You think he's cute." Jodie plinked out a few more bars of her new composition on the piano in the corner of the living room and turned to her sister, grinning that smirk of hers that Lauren knew was trouble.

Lauren sent her sister a warning look over her laptop. "I'd be lying if I said I didn't think he was attractive, but it's irrelevant." She turned her attention back to the purchase agreement the lawyers had drafted, sent to her by her future partner, Amy.

Part of her mind balked at the price tag, but it was an investment in building clients and staff. All of which would cost more to gather if they started from scratch.

"How is it irrelevant?" Jodie got up from the piano and fell onto the couch across from her. She dropped her feet on the coffee table, looking as if she was settling in for one of the heart-to-heart chats she loved.

"Don't put your feet on the table," Lauren chided.

"Don't be Dad," Jodie shot back, but her smile showed Lauren she hadn't taken her seriously.

Lauren sighed and closed her laptop. Clearly she wasn't getting anything done tonight.

"I think you should sell the ranch to Vic,"

Jodie said. "He's put a bunch of work into it and I'm sure he wants to buy it for Dean."

"I'm not averse to selling the ranch to him," Lauren said, slipping her reading glasses into their case. "If he can even match Alex Rossiter's offer, he can have it. But I doubt he can. When I told him what Alex was paying, I thought he would keel over."

Jodie twisted a strand of hair around her finger. Though her frown was partially hidden by her long bangs, it wasn't hard to read her dissatisfaction.

"I can tell you don't like the idea," Lauren continued. "I'm not alone in this, you know. The ranch is one-third yours."

"I know. Trouble is, I think you're right in saying that Vic can't match what Alex would pay you." Jodie took her feet off the table and set them on the couch, lounging sideways. "What does that Alex guy want with the ranch?"

"He owns property in the Caribbean and now he wants a ranch."

"A hobby ranch. To add to his collection." Jodie's voice held a faint sneer that Lauren chose to ignore. She wasn't wild about the idea, either. She would prefer to see it sold as a working ranch to someone personally invested in the property.

Someone like Vic.

"I think he sees the ranch as more of an investment," Lauren said. "But the stark reality is I need every penny of my third to buy into this new business. It's a huge opportunity I can't afford to let go. And if Vic needs the land base, he could lease it from Alex and run his cows."

"It's not the same. Alex would have all the control."

Lauren understood Jodie's concern. Wasn't that the very reason she was buying this business—so she could have control over her own life instead of depending on the whims of employers?

And worthless fiancés?

"I can't believe you would want to buy an accounting firm." Jodie shifted her position, curling her legs under her. She could never sit still long. "Why don't you just start your own accounting business? Just you. Why buy in to this one?"

"Because I need clients and I can't take any of the accounts I brought into Jernowicz Brothers or the last firm I worked at with me to a new business without being sued, and it would take too long to build up a new customer base. Even one-third of the amount Alex is willing to pay, after taxes, is barely enough for my buy-in. But I can't pass this up. It would mean a substantial income down the road, which means independence in many ways."

"And that's important to you." Jodie's words were more comment than condemnation.

It was important, Lauren thought, but not in the way that Jodie was implying. Not because money was the end-all and be-all for her.

After being dumped at the altar only to discover that she'd been lied to and milked dry by her ex-fiancé, then, in the past couple of months, fired by her most recent boss, Lauren needed some control in her life. Though Jodie knew about the canceled wedding, she knew little about the amounts of money Lauren had set aside to get the business she and Harvey had hoped to start on their own. She'd worked at Jernowicz Brothers, disliking every minute of the high-pressure job, while Harvey got things together for their eventual departure from the firm.

When he'd left her at the altar, he'd not only broken her heart, he had broken their bank account. The money they had set aside for the start of their new business had disappeared with him.

But she was too ashamed to tell Jodie that. She had always been the good example of what hard work could do. She wasn't about to share how badly Harvey had duped her.

With anyone.

"It's important to me to establish my independence," Lauren said instead. "I've lived enough of my life for other people—" She stopped there, not wanting Jodie to think that she resented the time she'd spent taking care of her. Taking care of their grandmother.

"You've done enough of that," Jodie agreed. "And I can understand that you'd want that, but I know enough of Vic that he wouldn't make this claim lightly. And if we find something to prove Vic's claim—" Jodie pressed, clearly unwilling to let this go.

"We haven't yet, and I doubt Dad would have hidden a paper like that away."

"He didn't exactly make the letters he wrote to us easy to find."

"They weren't hard to find, either," Lauren said, stifling a yawn. It had been a long, tiring day. Her head ached from thinking and phoning and planning and from reading her father's letters.

After his cancer diagnosis, their father had written each of the girls a letter apologizing for his behavior to them. It had been emotionally draining reading his words.

Though regret dogged her with every sentence her father had penned, she couldn't forget the tension that had held them all in a complicated grip each time they came to visit. He alternated between domineering and absent, angry and complacent. Though Lauren was sad he was gone, his loss didn't create the aching grief losing her mother and grandmother had.

But knowing that he did care, that he had felt bad about their relationship, had eased some of the residual bitterness from their time together.

"So what did you think about what Dad wrote?" Jodie asked. "Do you feel better about him now?"

Lauren reached over to the coffee table and picked up the handwritten letter Jodie had given her shortly after she'd arrived.

"I never had the issues with Dad that you did," Lauren said. "We never fought like you guys did, so I don't think I had as much to forgive him for. Knowing that he had sent money to Mom after their divorce helps. Mom always made it sound like he didn't support her and us at all. I don't want to get all psychoanalytical, but I think his absence in our lives, and how he treated us when we were here, had repercussions for all of us."

"Probably. Even Erin, who has always toed every line in her life, followed every rule without questioning, has had her relationship issues." Jodie shifted herself on the couch again. "I thought for sure she and that doctor guy she was dating would get married, but they broke up over half a year ago."

"She say anything to you about why they broke up?"

"Not a word. I know she's secretive, but she's been freaking me out with the radio silence she's been maintaining." Jodie sighed.

"I know, but at least she's staying in touch."

"If you want to call the occasional two-word text with emoticons staying in touch."

"It's better than nothing." Lauren had her own concerns about Erin, but she also knew her twin sister. Erin was a quiet and private person, something their ebullient younger sister didn't always understand. When she wanted to talk, she would. "You have Finn now, and it looks to me like you've found a place to settle after all the wandering you've been doing."

"I have. I've learned many things about myself over the years, and Finn has helped me through a lot. He makes me feel…complete. Loved. Treasured."

"I'm happy for you," Lauren said, trying hard to keep the note of envy out of her voice. She knew how unworthy Jodie had felt for much of her life. Lauren could identify all too well and was thankful her sister had found someone. Was thankful Jodie dared trust someone again.

She wasn't sure the same could happen to her.

"Oh, Lauren. I'm sorry," Jodie said, sitting up, instantly contrite. "I shouldn't be…all… happy and stuff."

"Of course you should," Lauren hastened to assure her. "I am happy for you. So happy. You had so many disappointments in your life. You deserve this."

"Don't know if *deserve* is the right word, but I am grateful," Jodie murmured. She gave Lauren a reassuring smile. "There's someone for you. I just know it."

"There might well be," Lauren said, crossing her arms over her chest. "But I don't want or need another relationship."

Jodie nodded, but Lauren saw her glance at the diamond ring on her finger. Her satisfied and peaceful smile created a nasty twist of jealousy.

At one time Lauren had worn a ring, too. At one time she had been making wedding plans.

She wasn't ready to go there again. Between her father's neglect and anger, and Harvey's lies, and her past bosses' treatment, she'd had enough.

But your father apologized.

She held that voice a moment, realizing that the apology had gone a long way to helping her settle the past.

However, he still had placed conditions on them. And as she fought a touch of resentment over that, a picture of Vic sitting across from her, holding her gaze, slipped into her mind. She knew Vic wasn't letting go of his claim on the ranch until he knew, without a doubt, that her father hadn't written anything up.

Which meant he would be around more than she liked. Not that she was attracted to him. She was never going down that road again.

Vic drove the tractor into the yard and pulled in front of Keith McCauley's shop, frustrated that he hadn't checked the amount of twine he had left in the baler before he started out this morning. He should have taken more with him, but he had been rushing all morning ever since he overslept.

Too much thinking last night, he told himself as he climbed out of the tractor. Too much on his mind. Dean. His widowed mother.

The missing deal with Keith. If he didn't find the papers, Lauren was ready to sell the ranch. At a price he couldn't afford.

He'd prayed about it and struggled to release it all into God's hands, but he kept pulling back.

Stay focused. You'll find the agreement.

He just wasn't sure when that was supposed to happen.

He stepped into the shop, the light from the open door slanting into the dark of the cool building. He blinked, letting his eyes adjust to the indoors from the bright sunlight outside.

But as he walked across the uneven concrete floor, he heard rustling and clanging coming from inside. He walked closer, listening. He reached for the door just as it opened under his hand.

Lauren stepped out carrying a shovel.

She wore blue jeans today and a dark T-shirt. Her hair hung in a loose braid over one shoulder, and as she looked up at him, the shovel fell to the floor with a clatter, her hand on her chest as she stumbled backward.

She would have fallen, but Vic caught her by one arm, pulling her upright. They stood that way a moment and he caught a whiff of her perfume.

She stared up at him, her eyes wide, a soft gray in the low light. There was a smudge of dirt on her cheek, some grass stuck in her hair.

"Oh. It's you," she said, breathless as she pulled away from him.

The speed with which she did it almost unbalanced her again, but this time she grabbed the door handle, looking hastily away.

"Yeah. I just needed some more twine for the baler." He poked his thumb over his shoulder. "Sorry I bothered you."

"No. No. That's fine. I just was startled. That's all." She pushed her hair back with the palm of her hand, creating another smudge of dirt. "I thought you were Jodie. She went to town and said she would be back soon."

With her blue jeans and casual shirt, dirty face and messy hair, she looked even more appealing than she normally did.

And he was, suddenly, not in any rush to find another roll of baler twine.

"You've got some dirt on your face," he said, pointing.

Lauren hastily scrubbed at her cheeks but only managed to make it worse.

Vic pulled out a hankie from his pocket and handed it to her. "Here. Use this."

She frowned as she looked down at the red polka-dotted square.

"I haven't used it yet," he assured her.

"Thanks, but that's not what I was worried about. I don't meet many men who actually use the hankies they carry." She hurriedly wiped her face, as if embarrassed he had caught her looking less than her best. "Though they're not called hankies, technically they're pocket squares and they're usually white, artfully folded and peeking out of a suit pocket." Then she released a short laugh. "Sorry. Babbling." She looked up at him, her expression questioning. "Did I get it all?"

"Still some on your left cheek," he said, pointing with his right hand. She wiped her right cheek. "No. The other left cheek," he said with a grin.

She wiped furiously at her left cheek but still missed the spot.

"A little more to the left," he said. A deep frown creased her forehead as she moved to the right, scrubbing again as if it was important she remove this dirt.

He finally took the hankie from her, caught her chin in his hand and wiped off the dirt himself. It was still smudged, but the worst was off.

He was disconcerted to see her looking up at him, her face holding a curious expression. "Sorry," he said, lowering his hands. "I thought…you…you'd…"

"No. Thanks. It's okay. I hate being dirty. Just a thing. Thanks."

"Well, if that's a problem, you've also got some grass in your hair." But this time, instead of explaining, he plucked it out himself.

"I guess I'm ready to face the world," she said with a nervous laugh, pulling away as he tugged at another piece.

As she did, his hand accidentally brushed her cheek, and she jumped as if he had struck her.

"Sorry," she said, sounding breathless as she leaned over to pick up the shovel. "Still jumpy. I wasn't expecting to see you."

"That was my fault. I didn't think anyone was in here, either. What are you doing with the shovel?"

"I'm cleaning out the flower beds. They're horribly overgrown. I used to take care of them every summer when we came to visit. Dad must have let them get out of hand."

"Your dad wasn't much for gardening," Vic said.

Lauren smiled at him and something dangerous shifted deep in his soul. He knew those first few whispers of attraction. Had felt them many times before. The last time was with Tiffany. Dean's ex-girlfriend.

The memory was like a slap and he knew he should leave. Yet, against his better judgment, he lingered.

"The lawn is crazy, as well," she continued as he mentally made his retreat from her. "I'm going to have to do three passes with the lawnmower before it's acceptable. And I'd like to go into town tomorrow to pick up some flowers. I think the greenhouse is still selling them."

"Why are you even bothering?" he asked, curiosity keeping him from stepping away. Curiosity and a deep loneliness that had been haunting him the past few months. He hadn't dated since Tiffany had told him she loved him. That she wanted to break up with Dean and get back together with him. They had dated previously, but she had broken up with him to date his brother. Then realized her mistake and wanted to get back together with Vic. He'd told her she had to do the right thing and tell his brother.

Her timing was atrocious. His inattention and Dean's anger had contributed to Dean's accident. Vic felt he was still paying for that mistake.

But now Lauren stood in front of him, attractive, appealing and, truth to tell, probably just as off-limits as Tiffany had been.

"Why bother?" she repeated with a gentle smile that didn't help his resolve. "It's something to do and, well, I'd like to make it nice for the future buyer."

Her words created a clench deep and low, bringing reality into their cozy little conversation.

"Of course. Good idea." He straightened his shoulders as if readying himself for whatever lay ahead. "I'll be done baling this field in a couple of hours. Would it be okay if I come inside and look through your father's papers afterward?"

"I'm meeting Keira Fortier for supper at the Grill and Chill tonight, so I don't think so."

"Another time, then?"

"Sure. When it works."

Vic fought down his frustration at her nonchalant attitude. This was as important to her as it was to him.

But she had choices.

He didn't.

Chapter Three

Vic lay on his back on the hay field, straining at the wrench. Grass slithered down his back as he wrestled with the bolt on the broken U joint connecting the PTO drive to the baler. Another day, another breakdown.

Yesterday he'd managed to get most of the one field baled. Today he wasn't sure he would get as much done.

Sweat streamed down his forehead into his eyes. It was hot and he was only half-done baling when the power take-off connecting the tractor to the baler rammed up.

He blinked and tugged again, pushing even harder. Finally the wrench moved. But his damp hands slid along the handle of the wrench banging into the shaft of the PTO, scraping the skin off his knuckles.

He sucked in a breath, allowed himself a

flash of self-pity, then picked up the wrench and got the bolt off, blood mingling with sweat on his hands.

He pulled the shaft of the PTO loose, ignoring the throbbing ache in his hands he finished the job.

He pulled out the broken U joint and got to his feet.

As he brushed dried grass off his shirt and pants, he stared at the clear blue sky that seemed to mock him. Hard to believe that rain would be pouring down tomorrow as the forecast on his phone showed. But he'd been fooled by that cloudless blue sky before, so he had to get to town as soon as possible, get the U joint welded, get back, fix it and get going until either evening dew or impending rain forced him to quit.

He shifted the U joint in his hands and trudged across the stubble of the hay field, thankful that the breakdown had happened so close to the yard. He saw his truck, parked now beside Lauren's car.

And beyond that, he saw Lauren working on the flower beds by the house.

Her car had been gone when he got here early this morning. Last night he hadn't had the opportunity to look for the agreement. So he had come early. But she hadn't been in the house this morning, either. Instead he'd gone directly to the tractor, hooked up the baler and gotten to work. She had returned about an hour ago. Now she was outside, working.

He climbed over the fence and headed toward his truck, wondering if he should stop and say hi.

Trouble was, he could still feel a flush of embarrassment at that little moment they had shared in the garage yesterday. He still wasn't sure what made him do it. He'd thought he was just being helpful, but when his hand brushed her cheek, a tiny shock had shot through him. Like electricity.

Like the feeling of a growing attraction he couldn't allow himself to indulge in.

He dropped the U joint into his jockey box at the back of the truck and was about to get in when he heard Lauren call his name, then saw her jog toward him.

As she came closer, he was unable to stop his heart lifting at the sight of her. Sandals and blue jeans again today, white tank top, hair tied back, tiny curls framing her flushed face.

She ran the back of her hand over her damp forehead as she stopped in front of him, breathless.

"Sorry to bother you. I was hoping to go

into town again this afternoon, but my car has a flat tire. Do you know whom I can call to get it fixed? Jodie is in Bozeman and not answering my calls. And Aunt Laura has been gone the past few days."

"I can change the tire for you."

"No. You've got your own work to do," Lauren said, turning down his offer with a flutter of her hands, her bright red nail polish flashing in the sun. "I don't want to be any trouble."

"If you've got a decent spare, it's no trouble."

"I should know how to do it myself, but living in the city…" She shrugged her shoulder. "I'd just call roadside assistance."

"Well, even if you called the tow truck, it could take a couple of hours before Dwayne got here." Vic gave her a crooked smile. "So, that leaves me, I guess. Unless you want to wait."

"I feel bad asking you."

Vic didn't even answer, just headed over to her car. The rim of the front driver's side tire was resting on the ground, the tire a puddle of rubber underneath it.

"Doesn't get much flatter," he said. "Where's your spare and jack?"

"All I know is that it's in the back. Sorry."

"No worries. I'll figure it out."

He opened the trunk and a few minutes later managed to finagle the full-size spare tire out of its compartment. When he dropped it on the ground, instead of a little bounce, it landed like a rock on its rim, as flat as the tire he was supposed to replace.

"Oh, no. I forgot that I'd already had a flat tire a couple of weeks ago," Lauren said with a note of disgust. "Stupid of me."

"I'm going into town now," Vic said. "I'll bring the tires in and get them fixed."

Lauren nodded, but Vic saw that she looked disappointed. Then he remembered. "You said you needed to go into town yourself. I can bring you where you want to go."

She hesitated, then gave him a sheepish smile. "That'd be great. I feel silly about that, too, because I was in town this morning and when I came home I realized I forgot some groceries."

"Get in. I'll drop you off and get your tire fixed."

"I just need to change, if that's okay."

"No problem," he said, though he wondered why. He thought she looked fine.

Of course he wasn't one to judge what was suitable, he thought, glancing down at his grease-stained blue jeans and dirty shirt.

He manhandled the tires into the back of the truck, getting even more dirt on his shirt. He called the machine shop to see if he could get the part in, and thankfully they could repair it while he waited.

He brushed some hay off his shirt, beat his dusty cowboy hat against his leg and ran his fingers through his tangled hair. That was about as changed as he was getting.

A few moments later Lauren came down the walk and Vic felt even shabbier. She wore a blue-striped button-down shirt, narrow black skirt and white canvas shoes. Her hair was pulled back again into a ponytail and she had even put on some makeup.

In a mere ten minutes she had transformed from a country girl to a city slicker.

"We'll bring your tires in first, then I'll need to drop my part off at the machine shop, if that's okay," Vic said as they got into the truck.

"You're doing me a huge favor. I can hardly dictate the terms of the arrangement," Lauren said, setting her purse on her lap.

Vic acknowledged that with a nod, then headed down the driveway toward the gravel road and town.

"I noticed you were haying. How many acres of the ranch are in hay?" Lauren asked.

"About two hundred and fifty." He wondered why she asked.

"Is that a lot?"

"It's enough to keep my cows in feed. My dad and I turned our own hay fields on the ranch into pasture, because the land here is more fertile and gets me better yields."

"But there is some pasture here?"

"Oh, yeah. I run some cows here, too. Mostly up in the high pasture behind the ranch and across the road."

"I see." Lauren folded her hands on her purse and gave him a quick glance. "Sounds kind of silly that I know so little about the ranch. I never paid much attention to it. Erin was the one who liked to help. She'd spend hours wandering the back fields and occasionally working with our father."

"I remember Erin. She was a sweet girl."

"Very sweet. Hard to believe we were twins. She always made me try to be a better person. Somehow, she was the only one of us girls who got along with our father when we came back here. She never resented leaving Knoxville like Jodie and I did."

He kept his eyes on the road, but half of his attention was on Lauren.

"So you didn't like it here?" he asked. "Coming every summer?"

"I missed my friends back home and I always felt bad leaving Gramma behind, but there were parts I liked."

"I remember seeing you girls in church on Sunday." Jodie had usually worn some goofy outfit that Vic was sure Keith had vetoed, Erin a ruffly dress and Lauren the same simple clothes she favored now.

"Part of the deal," Lauren said, but a faint smile teased one corner of her mouth. "And I didn't mind that part, either. I liked hearing Aunt Laura play, and the message was always good, once I started really listening. I can't remember who the pastor was at that time, but much of what he said resonated with me."

"Jodie and Erin would attend some of the youth events, didn't they?"

"Erin more than any of us. Like I said, she was the good girl."

"I remember my brother, Dean, talking about her," Vic said, surprised to see her looking at him. "I think he had a secret crush on her."

"He was impetuous, wasn't he?"

"That's being kind. He was out of control for a while. But he's settled now."

Vic thought of the journey Dean had made to get to where he was. Which brought up the same pressing problem that had brought him early to the ranch.

His deal with Keith.

"So, I hate to be a broken record," he continued, "But it's supposed to rain tomorrow. I was wondering if I could come by the house then? To go through your father's papers?"

Lauren's sigh was eloquent as was the way her hands clasped each other tightly.

Vic tamped down his immediate apology. He had nothing to feel bad about. He was just doing what he'd promised himself he'd do after Dean's accident. Looking out for his brother's interests.

"Yes. Of course. Though—" She stopped herself there. "Sorry. You probably know better what you're looking for."

Vic shot her a glance across the cab of the truck. "I'm not trying to be ornery or selfish or jeopardize your deal. When I first leased the ranch from your father, it was so that my brother could have his own place. And I'm hoping to protect that promise I made him. Especially now. After his accident."

Lauren's features relaxed enough that he assumed he was getting through to her.

"I'm sorry. I understand," she said, her smile apologetic. "I know what it's like to protect siblings. I did plenty of that in my life."

"Are you the oldest?"

"Erin and I are twins, but I'm older by twenty minutes. And you?"

"The same. So yeah, I hear you on the protecting the younger ones."

Lauren smiled back at him. And as their eyes held, he felt it again. An unexpected and surprising rush of attraction. When her eyes grew ever so slightly wider and her head lowered just a fraction, he wondered if she felt it, too.

He dragged his attention back to the road and fought down the emotions.

You're no judge of your feelings, he reminded himself, his hands tightening on the steering wheel as if reining in his attraction to this enigmatic woman.

He'd made mistakes in the past, falling for the wrong person. He couldn't do it again. He couldn't afford to.

Especially not with Lauren.

"You can still plant these this year, but you won't see them flower fully until next season."

The young girl wearing a green apron, a huge smile and a smudge of dirt on her neck held up the pot holding the spiky-leafed lily. She turned it as if checking it from all angles.

"It's a stargazer and they tend to bloom a little later in the season than the Asiatic does."

The warm afternoon sun filtered through the greenhouse, creating a tropical warmth. Plants in full bloom filled most of the wooden benches with swaths of pink and yellow petunias, the delicate blue, lavender and white of the lobelia, the hard red, salmon, white and pink of geraniums. People filled the aisles, talking, comparing, and laughing. A few people had greeted Lauren, some she recognized, but she couldn't pull their names out of her memory.

The atmosphere in this place was one of quiet and peace. As she drew in a deep breath of the peaty scent, a sense of expectation thrummed through her. Though it was getting close to the end of the planting season, the shop still had a lot of stock.

"Which color is this lily?"

"This is the deep pink one. The flowers are edged with white and the spots on them are a darker shade of pink. They smell heavenly, though some people find it strong."

The young girl, Nadine, had been a veritable font of information. Lauren found herself wandering deeper and deeper into the greenhouse and buying far more plants than she had anticipated.

She had quickly gotten her groceries, and instead of waiting, had come into the greenhouse, which was right beside the grocery store.

And then she met Nadine, and here she was, eight pots and seven twelve-packs of flowers later. Helping her aunt in her flower shop had given Lauren some knowledge. Though she knew little about bedding out plants and perennials, she was learning.

She shot a quick glance at her watch. Vic had said he would meet her in front of the store at two. It was only one forty-five.

"They come in white, as well," Nadine said. "Just think how nice they could look together. A cluster of white in the middle of a bunch of pink. You'd have to buy more than one white, though."

"You're bad for my wallet, girl," Lauren chided as she picked up the tag attached to the plant Nadine had pointed out. It showed a large white six-petaled flower with ruffled edges. She was imagining them in the rock garden that edged the deck. Neither she nor her sisters had met their father's mother who, apparently, was an avid gardener when she lived on the ranch.

Lauren's mother had never been interested in gardening, and when Lauren and her sisters had visited the ranch, they'd been too young to care.

"Did you get your grocery shopping done?"

The deep voice behind her made her jump and Lauren spun around to see Vic standing there, thumbs hanging above the large buckle of his belt. He had rolled up the sleeves of his stained twill shirt, the hat pulled over his head now tipped to one side.

His mouth curved in a laconic smile, but she easily saw the warmth of his eyes.

She swallowed, frustrated again at the effect this man had on her.

"Yes. I put the bags close to the entrance," she said. "One of the cashiers said she would watch them for me."

"They're in the truck already," he said, shifting his weight to his other leg. "Sonja told me you were in here and that you'd left her in charge of your food."

She had felt strange enough leaving her groceries with the chatty woman at the front desk who assured her she wouldn't eat her food. But then to have Vic simply load them in the truck?

"Everyone knows everyone in Saddlebank and even worse, everyone's business," he said, his grin deepening. "Am I right, Nadine?" he asked the greenhouse clerk, winking at her.

The girl blushed, looking down at the pot she still held, turning it over. "Yeah. Well. That's Saddlebank." She gave Vic another shy glance, her flush growing.

Nice to know she wasn't the only one he had this effect on, Lauren thought, reminding herself to stay on task. To keep her focus.

You have your own plans. He's just a hindrance and a distraction.

A good-looking distraction, she conceded, but a distraction nonetheless.

"So what do you all have here?" he asked, pointing to the plants.

"Gerberas, lilies, petunias, some marigolds. Lobelia, geraniums and million bells—"

"Gotcha," he said, holding his hands up as if to stop her, looking somewhat overwhelmed. "Do you need help packing these up?"

Lauren glanced from the wagon holding the flowers she had chosen to the rest of the greenhouse. She could spend another hour wandering, planning and dreaming, but she had taken up enough of Vic's time and she knew he was anxious to get back to work.

"I have to pay for them first," she said. She turned the cart around and walked down the wooden aisles to the checkout counter.

But her feet slowed as she passed a preplanted pot of pink and purple million bells, white lobelia, trailing sweet potato vine and yellow aspermums. She pinched off a dead flower, her hand arranging the one vine.

"That's pretty," Vic said, his voice holding a note of approval.

"I love the colors they've used. It would look lovely on a deck." Then she pulled her hand back, knowing that she had already spent more than she should, and marched on, resisting the temptation.

She got to the cashier, unloaded her plants on the old wooden counter, pulled her debit card out of her wallet and slapped it on the counter as if afraid her more practical self would convince her it was a waste of money.

"You've got some lovely plants." Sonja bustled about as she rang them up on the old-fashioned cash register, her gray curls bouncing. She was an older woman, with a rough voice and a broad smile. Her T-shirt proclaimed Life's a Garden. Dig It. "If you need any help or advice, you just call. We can answer all your questions. 'Course, you have your aunt to help you out. I know you used to help her at the flower shop from time to time," she said.

"I'm sorry, I feel like I should remember you," Lauren said.

"I used to deliver perennial pots to your aunt's shop," Sonja said. "Used to see you and your sisters there once in a while."

Then Lauren did remember. Sonja was always laughing and joking, her personality filling the store, making it a fun and happy place to be.

But before Lauren could say anything, Sonja was finished with her and already on to the next customer. Lauren looked around for Vic, doing a double take as she realized he was purchasing the pot she had just admired.

"Figured if you liked it, so would my mom," he said as he pulled his wallet out of his back pocket.

"Your mother will love them." Sonja rang up his purchase, smiling her approval. "Very considerate of you."

"I'm angling for son of the year," Vic said.

"And he'll get it, don't you think, Lauren?"

"I guess" was all Lauren could muster. She was still wrapping her head around a guy buying a potted plant for his mother.

"Our Vic is an amazing young man," Sonja said, her voice heavy with meaning. She gave Lauren a knowing look that she didn't have to interpret. "A girl would be lucky to have him."

"I think it's time to load up what we got

and get out of here," Vic cut in with a sheepish smile as he set the pot he'd just bought on the two-layered cart holding Lauren's plants.

"You know I'm right," Sonja teased, looking from Vic to Lauren as if connecting the two. "You won't find better in all of Saddlebank."

"Now it's really time to go," Vic said, ushering Lauren out of the store. His truck was right out the door and he opened the back door of the double cab. "If it's okay with you, I thought we could set them here," he said as he started unloading them.

"But you'll get the floor of your truck dirty," Lauren protested. The carpet was immaculately clean and the seats even more so.

"It's honest dirt," he said, tossing her a grin as he took the pots from her and set them on the carpet. "Sorry about Sonja, by the way. She's the local busybody."

"I remember her coming into my aunt's flower shop," Lauren said. Sonja's comment had made her even more aware of Vic than she liked. "She was like this ball of energy."

"That about sums her up." He got into the truck. "Do you need to do anything else?"

"I think I've taken enough of your time and spent enough of my money. I know you want to get back to your hay baling."

"Yeah. I do. Thanks."

A few minutes later they were back on the highway, headed toward the ranch. Lauren's groceries were stashed on the floor of the truck by her feet.

"By the way, I can't thank you enough for taking care of the tires," Lauren said. "But shouldn't we have stopped to pay for them?"

"You can next time you're in town. I talked to Alan, who runs the place. He said it was okay."

Lauren shook her head. "Small towns," she said. "I can't imagine getting away with running a business like that in Boston or Fresno."

"You lived in both those places?"

"And Chicago, and New York for a month. I live in Charlotte, North Carolina, now."

"That's a lot of moving."

"Harvey, my fiancé was a real go-getter. Always looking for a better job."

"And you followed him around?"

"Sort of. His opportunities were good for me, as well." She was surprised at how his comment made her feel.

"Your dad said you worked as an accountant."

Lauren chuckled at the grimace on his face. "It's good work."

Vic shuddered. "Numbers are not my

friends. I can't imagine working with them all day."

"To each his own," she said. "I like how predictable and orderly they make life. There's no surprises or guesswork. One plus one will always equal two."

"Do you enjoy it? Is it your passion?"

Lauren opened her mouth to say yes but hesitated. To say it was her passion wasn't correct. "I'm good at it and it pays well."

Vic laughed and she shot him a puzzled glance. "Is it the money? That why you do it? You don't seem like that kind of person."

Lauren's back stiffened. "No. Of course not. I do it because I'm competent. I'm trained for it and because…because…well…I've got this opportunity now to start my own business and…" For a few long moments she couldn't latch on to any solid reason why. No one had ever asked her. Harvey had always assumed this was what she should do.

She turned away from Vic and his probing questions and curious expression. The uncertainty his comments raised frustrated her. Then came a chilling realization.

It's because that's all you've ever done.

"I'm sorry if I've upset you," Vic said. "I was just making conversation."

She suddenly felt as if the ground that she

had always thought of as solid and unmoving had shifted.

You don't seem like that kind of person.

How did he know what she was like?

"It's all right," she said, giving him a careful smile. "For some reason your comment caught me unawares."

"Never a good place to be caught," Vic said. "I'm sorry."

"No. Please don't apologize. If I'm honest, money is part of it, that's true enough. There never was enough when I was growing up. I remember reading the beatitudes and Jesus saying, 'Blessed are the poor,' and I thought he was wrong. There was no blessing in being broke. There was no honor in buying clothes from a thrift store and getting teased about them. Jodie managed to find her own style. But I used to be ashamed that my clothes were secondhand, and Gramma chastised me many times for that. She often made me feel guilty that I wanted more. Even Dad would tell me not to be so proud."

"Keith was a frugal man."

"That's a kind way of saying he was stingy."

Vic gave her another one of his killer smiles that touched her soul.

"So what was your passion when you were

younger?" he pressed. "What did you always want to do? Where were you the happiest?"

Lauren considered his questions. "You know, my favorite times were when I was in my aunt's flower shop. My dad would send us there once in a while when he didn't know what else to do with us. I loved working with the flowers. I loved watching my aunt arrange them and combine colors and textures and create interesting displays. When I was older, she let me try my hand at it." She released a light laugh. "I think the true appeal of my aunt's shop was the calm I felt there. The happiness. It was like a little sanctuary for me and my sisters."

"Sounds like it was a good place for you."

A memory floated upward and she caught it. "When I was eighteen, my last summer here, I remember my aunt suggesting that I stay in Saddlebank and help her in the flower shop."

"So why didn't you?"

"My grandmother became ill and she needed me back in Knoxville."

"And being the responsible person you are, you went and you took care of her."

"I owed her a lot. Erin had just been accepted at college, and I wasn't sure what I wanted to do and hadn't applied anywhere, so I figured it was best if I stay. Jodie was only sixteen and still in high school. Someone needed to help Gramma."

Vic looked at her with a fleeting sadness. "That's quite a sacrifice for such a young girl. And quite amazing."

She heard warmth, approval and sympathy in his voice, and for some reason, it made her feel emotional.

"She'd given us a home. It was the least I could do."

"And now, this business you're buying?"

His question lingered as if he wasn't sure what he wanted to ask about it. She knew her decision was the reason she was selling the ranch and that it had a huge impact on him, but she had to stay the course.

"It's an opportunity. A good one. The woman I'm partnering with is energetic and hardworking, and I think this is a good chance for me to strike out on my own."

"Working with numbers every day."

"You don't need to make it sound like a death sentence," she added with a light laugh. "I'm good at it and this business I'm buying in to is a…I think this is a good opportunity. A chance to take care of myself."

"But I understand you'll be doing that with a partner."

"Yes, but she's someone I can trust."

You thought you could trust Harvey. You thought you could trust your boss.

The words slammed into her and she had to clench her fists to control the anger that rose within her.

Even as she spoke she found herself reaching. As if she had to convince herself as much as him.

"And what about you," she countered, tired of analyzing her own life. "What's your passion?"

"Ranching. Always ranching," he said, his voice strong with a conviction that she envied. "That's never changed. My dad worked the ranch I live on and his grandfather before that and his grandfather before that. We're not as old as the Bannister ranch, but close. It's my heritage and I love it." He gave her a sheepish smile. "I'm just a basic guy. A cattleman born and bred."

"You're fortunate to have that legacy," she said, wondering if she could ever muster up the same passion for her work that seemed to be ingrained into his identity. Her work was something she'd stumbled into. Something she discovered she was competent at, and her career carried on from there.

For a moment, however, she wondered

what her life would have been like if she'd followed through on Aunt Laura's suggestion. If she'd stayed in Saddlebank.

It was a moot point, she reminded herself. Her grandmother had needed her.

But still…

"Your dad's ranch goes back a few generations, as well," Vic said, breaking into her thoughts.

"Dad was never as much a rancher as you seem to be," Lauren said. "I think he only did it because he inherited it from his father. And though we stayed there, it never felt… like home. I always felt more like a guest in some ways."

"Did Knoxville feel like home?"

"Kind of. But there at least we were at our grandmother's home. She was kind enough, but it was still her place."

"So, no real home base? That's sad."

Lauren glanced over at him, surprised at his sympathy, surprised to see him looking at her.

Their gazes held, and when Vic smiled, once again she felt connection and possibilities. Her breath seemed hard to find and an unusual urge to reach across the truck overcame her. To touch his hand.

Her cell phone rang and he jerked his head

aside. Lauren crashed back down to earth when she glanced at the name flashing on the screen.

Alex Rossiter. The ranch's potential buyer.

"Hello, Alex," she said, disappointed at how breathless she sounded. "What can I do for you?"

"Was wondering if I could come by next week Tuesday," he said, his voice booming in her ear. Alex was a large man with a large voice and matching attitude. "To look over the place. See what I'm getting into."

As he spoke Lauren drew in a shaky breath, feeling as if she had to find her balance.

"I think that should work," she said.

They made arrangements, but all the while she talked, she couldn't help feeling guilty. As if she was doing something wrong.

Alex abruptly said goodbye and Lauren lowered her phone, trying to find the right way to tell Vic what was happening. Straightforward was always best, she decided.

"That was the buyer of the ranch," she said, turning to Vic. "He wants to come out on Tuesday."

Vic just nodded, his jaw tight, his eyes narrowed as he stared straight ahead.

She put her phone in her purse and folded her hands on her lap, staring out the window.

But as they drove back to the ranch, she couldn't shake the sensation that she had caught a glimpse of another life. A life that held light and joy.

She shook off the capricious emotion.

She had a good plan. She had to stick with it. How it affected Vic shouldn't matter to her.

In spite of his approval of what she had done for her grandmother, it was a reminder of the many times she had put other people first in her life.

It was time to take care of herself.

Chapter Four

"My girls." Aunt Laura tugged a green apron over her purple tunic as she grinned at Lauren and Jodie. The three of them had gathered in the back room of her florist shop to discuss the flowers for Jodie's wedding. "I'm so excited to help with this," she said, tugging on gloves before she pulled some white roses out of the large plastic tub. She laid them on the large butcher-block table, then pulled another tub closer to her.

The store was closed and after they were done Lauren knew they would be invited for tea. It was a ritual played out many times in their childhood when the girls were on their own because their father was busy with haying.

As Vic had been the past few days.

An image of Vic slipped into Lauren's

mind along with their conversation in the truck yesterday. It had been a long time since she'd spent any amount of time with a man in a relaxed setting. He seemed like a nice guy and she regretted the fact that she couldn't sell the ranch to him.

He had come to the house again this afternoon but had spent most of that time in the office. For which she was thankful. Being around him made her nervous.

A phone call from his brother cut his time short, and with an apology and a request to come back, he had left.

Trouble was, she and Jodie were going to Bozeman for the next few days to look at wedding and bridesmaid dresses and wouldn't be home.

"Lauren, can you grab some of those bells of Ireland?" Aunt Laura asked as she pulled some delphinium out of a tub.

Lauren frowned at her aunt's selection.

"Are you sure?" she asked, trying to visualize how the combination would look.

"Yes. Why?" The look that accompanied her aunt's question told Lauren that she had noticed Lauren's lapse and was wondering about it.

"Nothing. Just curious," she said, giving a quick smile that dismissed her aunt's curiosity. She didn't want to get into a discussion about Vic with her aunt and her sister present. She knew exactly what they would think.

Lauren entered the back cooler, enjoying the rainbow colors of roses, forsythia, tulips and dozens of other flowers whose names she slowly recalled. There in one corner, she caught the distinctive green of the bells of Ireland. She grabbed the container, shivering as she closed the cooler behind her.

"Now I know these aren't often put together in a bouquet," Aunt Laura said as she tugged a few out of the tub and slipped them into an arrangement. "But I think it could look dramatic. What do you think, Jodie?"

"I like it," Jodie said, but Lauren sensed she wasn't enthusiastic.

Aunt Laura tugged some baby's breath and wove it in.

"This might help," she said with a hopeful note.

"That does soften it a little."

But the forced smile told Lauren that Jodie had a different vision.

Lauren gathered up some of the discarded roses and lilies. She wove in some pussy willows and few hyacinths and added boronia, a cluster of small bell-like flowers.

"Oh, what's that?" Jodie said, moving over to where Lauren worked. "That's awesome."

"Oh, I was just fooling around," Lauren said, setting the bouquet on the table, self-conscious.

Her aunt looked from the flowers she had just put together, then at Lauren's bouquet. "You always did have a good eye for composition. I remember when you worked here, I couldn't keep up with the demand for your arrangements."

Lauren wiped her hands on her slacks. "It's fun. I just like trying different combinations."

"What would you do for bridesmaids?" Aunt Laura asked.

"I was just experimenting. You're the florist."

"And you're the one with talent. I'd like to see what else you would do." Aunt Laura's bright smile showed Lauren that she wasn't hurt. In fact, she seemed interested.

"Okay. How about we do this." Lauren reluctantly reached down to a tub of peonies and made a tight bouquet with them. She added a couple of the roses and some baby's breath this time. "This is a rough idea. We could frame it with banana leaves or, if you want to go more girly, with a circle of tulle."

"Oh, I like that," Jodie breathed, suddenly more animated.

"See, you have the gift," Aunt Laura said. "I think we should talk about you helping me out with the wedding flowers."

Lauren wasn't sure she would be able to help much. She would be in the middle of setting up her new business right before the wedding.

But as she looked over the flowers on the table, she felt a yearning she couldn't ignore. "We'll see" was all she said.

"And now I think we need to have tea."

They followed their aunt up the back stairs to her apartment. A few moments later they sat around her dining room table, munching on sugar cookies.

The lights were turned low, and the classical music Aunt Laura loved played softly in the background. For the first time since she'd come back to Saddlebank, Lauren felt at ease. Comfortable. Relaxed.

"So, tell me, have you girls heard anything from Erin yet?" Aunt Laura asked, sitting down across from them, her gray hair cut in a bob, her eyes looking from one to the other.

"I tried to call her, but she didn't answer her phone," Lauren said. "She sent me a text shortly after, though. She's been busy. At least that's her excuse."

"I'm just wondering why she won't talk to us," Jodie said, stirring yet another spoonful of sugar into her tea. "It's like she's avoiding us."

"She used to do that more often," Aunt Laura said, wiping a crumb of sugar from her lips. "I remember these intentional forays into melancholy she used to indulge in. She always was more introverted than either of you girls."

"I remember Dad getting so ticked at her when she would wander off into the hills and not come back for hours." Jodie released a light laugh that held little humor. "He could be so hard-nosed."

"Jodie. Careful," Lauren reprimanded. "Don't speak—"

"Ill of the dead," Jodie chimed in, giving her sister a sly wink to show her that her comment didn't bother her. "Gramma's mantra. I know, but it's still hard. Even in spite of the letters of apology he wrote both of us."

"Your father had his…moments," Aunt Laura said. "I just wish you could have spoken to him before he died. Gotten some of this stuff out of the way."

"Would he have said in person the things

he wrote in our letters?" Lauren asked, taking a sip of her tea.

"Maybe. The actual words of apology were hard for him. He would do other things to show he was sorry." Aunt Laura gave them a sorrowful smile. "I hope you can appreciate that the letters he wrote you were a big deal for him. I know he spent hours sitting at his table in the café writing them. I hope it gives you a different view of him and, at the same time, a different view of the ranch. It's been in the family for decades."

Guilt suffused Lauren at her aunt's offhand comment.

"I know it's been handed down through the generations and I'm sorry none of us will be taking it over." Lauren glanced over at Jodie. "Finn doesn't want it, and well…" She let her comment fade away, not sure she wanted her aunt to know how important the money was to her.

Aunt Laura waved her hands as if erasing what she had just said. "I wasn't saying you need to hang on to it just because it's a family heirloom. I want you to have some good memories of your father here. It was a part of your life and it's a good place. I know I have good memories from living there. I just wanted to know that you did, too."

Her aunt looked so distressed Lauren clasped her aunt's hands between hers to reassure her. "It's okay, Auntie. I do have good memories. It's just…"

"I'm so sorry I brought it up," Aunt Laura said. "I know your father was hard to live with. And, well, he had his reasons."

"Jodie told me you read her letter," Lauren said.

"Yes. I did."

"I hope that's okay," Jodie said to her. "Auntie was visiting one afternoon and it was on the table."

"Of course it is," Lauren said. "It was yours to show to whoever you wanted. But I guess I was thinking of what Dad said in Jodie's letter. About Mom cheating on him. Was that true?"

Aunt Laura pushed a few granules of sugar that had fallen off her napkin into a tiny pile as she seemed to ponder what Lauren had said.

"It was," she said. "Your mother wasn't a happy wife."

"Why not?"

"Your father never said anything in your letter, Lauren? About his marriage?"

"It was a lot of the same stuff that he told Jodie. That he was sorry he wasn't a better father. He said something in mine about his own struggles and he did say that he suspected Mom had cheated on him."

"I never wanted to say anything to you girls, and the truth was, it didn't matter so much." Aunt Laura carefully added a few more granules to her pile. "Your parents were already divorced. Like your grandmother said, I didn't want to cast any aspersions on your mother's character by speaking ill of the dead. But I think you need to know that your parents had to get married," she said.

"Had to?" Lauren's question broke into her aunt's statement. "As in, she was pregnant?"

"With you and Erin," Aunt Laura said, giving her an apologetic smile. "Your mom had just moved to Saddlebank and needed a job. I hired her at the flower shop and introduced them. She was fun and vivacious, and Keith, well, he'd always leaned toward the darker side, so I thought she would be good for him. Keith liked your mother well enough, but I don't think he ever planned to marry her. He had his own dreams. After our father died, Keith wanted to sell the ranch and join the marines. But when he found out your mother was expecting, he stepped up to his responsibilities. In retrospect, while it seemed the right thing to do at the time, it might not have been the best decision for either of them."

Aunt Laura paused, and Lauren glanced over at Jodie, gauging her reaction. She looked just as stunned as she felt.

"The cracks in their marriage started showing right away. They got worse after you were born," Aunt Laura continued, looking from one sister to the other. "Your mother would drive to Bozeman and go shopping, spending money your father didn't have. Your father wasn't a cattleman. He inherited the ranch from our father, so he rented it out and started working for the county as a sheriff's deputy. He loved his job. It was the closest he ever came to becoming a marine. But he didn't make a lot of money, so that caused other problems."

Lauren listened, trying to process what Aunt Laura was saying. She tried to balance it with her own memories of her mother, a sad woman who often complained about their father.

"Was their marriage all bad?" Jodie asked.

"No, honey. Not all bad." Aunt Laura gave both of them a smile. "Your father did love his family. And while he loved being in Saddlebank, ranching wasn't his first love. So I don't know if this helps you see your father in a different light. I'm hoping it makes you all a bit more sympathetic toward him. He may not have been the nicest person, but he was my brother and I miss him."

Lauren heard the choked note in her aunt's voice and both she and Jodie reached across the table and took her hand.

"Of course you do," Lauren assured her. "We do, too."

Aunt Laura gave them both a wavery smile. "I don't want to put anything more on your shoulders or influence your decision. I know you have your reasons and I'm sure they're good ones, but I am going to be sorry to see the ranch go to a stranger." She sat up and pushed her chair away. "And now we've had our confession time. You get to see a side of your parents you never did and I got to unload a secret that should have been told a long time ago. I think this calls for another cup of tea and some more cookies."

After she walked away, Lauren looked at Jodie, who had a puzzled expression on her face.

"Do we really need to do this?" Jodie whispered, leaning closer to Lauren.

"Do what?"

"Sell the ranch to that guy?"

"I'm not going to run it, you said Finn

wasn't interested, and we both know Vic can't pay what Alex is offering. Besides, does it really matter who owns the ranch?" Lauren whispered back, shooting a quick glance to the kitchen, where Aunt Laura was making a fresh pot of tea. "You're established, Erin doesn't seem to want to come back and I'll be gone."

"I know. That's part of the problem."

"I'm not a rancher," Lauren murmured. "And I've no intention of becoming one. And while I'd love to stick around—"

"Would you?" Jodie asked, a pained note in her voice. "Would you really?"

"I would. Really," Lauren said, stroking her sister's shoulder. "I would love to be close to you. But I need to be realistic. I need to make a living. Take care of myself."

"I thought the same thing," Jodie said. "And then I met Finn."

"Well, you were lucky. I don't see that in my future."

"What about Vic?"

Lauren gave her sister an *oh, really* look that hopefully dismissed that idea. Then she smiled as their aunt came into the room, bearing a tray with more cookies and a fresh pot of tea.

"Are you talking about Vic Moore?" Aunt Laura asked.

"Yes."

"No."

Jodie and Lauren spoke at the same time.

"He's a wonderful young man," Aunt Laura said, ignoring Lauren's comment. "And so handsome and kind and loyal." She eased out a sigh. "I used to have the biggest crush on his father. He was just as good-looking. Just as nice."

"So why didn't you go for him?" Jodie asked, unwilling to let go of the topic of the Moore family.

"He had eyes only for Trudy, his wife." Aunt Laura sighed. "But Vic is still single, I understand," she said, looking over at Lauren. "He would make a fine husband."

"Nice try, Auntie," Lauren said. "But I think I'll pass. I need to focus on my business. That's my future." Last night she had called her partner, Amy, and listening to her enthusiasm for their new business had helped ground her back in reality.

"Be careful," Aunt Laura warned. "A business can be fulfilling, but I wouldn't want you to miss out on love."

"Love is overrated," Lauren said. But even as she dismissed her aunt's comment, she wondered if Aunt Laura was talking about her own life and running her flower shop.

"And how is your work with Maddie Cole going?" Aunt Laura asked Jodie, as Lauren poured them all more tea.

Maddie was a professional singer Jodie had accompanied at a concert held before Lauren came to the ranch. Maddie had been so enthusiastic about a composition Jodie had written, they'd been working together since then.

"We're working on a new set of songs that she wants to record, but I'm having trouble with a transition in one of them. Lauren and I are going to Bozeman tomorrow, and I'll stay a few more days after that to work with her. But I'd like to have it figured before I go. Maybe you could help me?"

"Sure. Let's go to the piano."

Jodie and Aunt Laura stood up, and Lauren grabbed a couple of cookies and followed them to the living room, dropping onto the couch. She munched on a cookie, happy to listen to her sister and aunt talk music.

But in spite of her resolve, as she listened to Jodie and Aunt Laura trying out a new melody, a dull lonely ache clenched her heart.

Her aunt had warned her not to miss out on love. So why did a picture of Vic shift into her mind? Too easily she remembered his gentle touch as he wiped the mud off her face. The crook of his smile that, somehow, didn't make her feel embarrassed at all.

She pushed the thoughts aside.

Don't go there. You have your plans. They're enough, and no man is worth sacrificing them for.

The noise of the people gathering in the fellowship hall of the church washed over Vic as he walked through the open double doors. He would have preferred to go directly home after church, but he had driven his mother to the service this morning and she'd expressed a desire to stay and chat.

Kids ran between adults, shrieking their pleasure as they played hide-and-seek or tag or whatever game they needed to burn off energy after sitting quiet for the past hour.

A little boy zipped past him, catching his toe in the carpet. He would have fallen if Vic hadn't caught him by the arm.

"Hey, little guy, you might want to slow down."

The little boy, his hair sticking up in spikes, his plaid shirt open over a juice-stained T-shirt, flashed a gap-toothed grin at him, then ran off. A child on a mission.

Vic chuckled as he walked over to the table

where a huge urn sat, and poured himself some coffee. He glanced around the people milling about, laughing and talking, his eyes unconsciously searching the crowd for a certain tall blonde woman who had attended church today.

According to Jodie, Lauren wasn't the most faithful churchgoer, so when he saw her come in and sit down in the spot where her father used to sit, across from where his parents always sat, he couldn't help a second look. He knew she and Jodie had been in Bozeman the past few days, so he was surprised to see her at all.

Trouble was, he glanced over the same time she did. He knew he didn't imagine the faint stir of connection between them. Or the fact that she didn't look away right away, either.

"So how is the haying going?"

Vic glanced up from his coffee just as Lee Bannister joined him.

Tall, with dark hair and deep-set, intent brown eyes, a square jaw and a demeanor that commanded respect, Lee tended to stand out in a crowd. But Vic knew him to be a humble, caring man who had learned some hard life lessons.

"Coming along. The usual dog and pony show. Breakdowns and rain. But we should be okay. I'm cutting again tomorrow." Vic stirred his coffee and set the used spoon in a bowl. "But should be a good crop."

"You put up hay on the McCauley place, don't you?" Lee asked as he poured some coffee for himself. "I heard you've been leasing it. How will that work now that Keith's dead and the girls own the ranch? You able to make a deal with them?"

"It's all up in the air right now," he admitted, taking a sip of his coffee, wishing he could get a break from his own spinning thoughts.

"That's got to make your plans complicated. I know you had figured on that place for Dean."

"I did." Vic shrugged. "I guess I'll just have to take the pastor's words to heart."

This morning the pastor had preached on the need to trust and let go of the desire to control one's own life. Vic knew, especially the past few weeks, that he struggled with precisely that. It was hard to let go when his own brother depended on him to help.

"Don't we all," Lee said with a light sigh. "I know I've had to learn to let go of my own plans."

Vic nodded, acknowledging the wisdom he was sure Lee had gleaned from his time in prison for a crime he didn't commit. Yet the man wasn't bitter. In fact he seemed downright happy.

Probably had something to do with the pretty redhead who joined them. Abby Bannister granted Vic a quick greeting then gently tugged on Lee's arm.

"Sorry to interrupt, but I just got a call," she said. "That photo shoot I had planned for later this afternoon got bumped up and I have to leave right away."

"Of course. Let's go." Lee set his mug down and gave Vic a warm smile, clapping his hand on his shoulder. "I sure hope things turn out for you and Dean. He's had a rough go."

"He has," Vic agreed. "Take care."

As Lee left, Vic suddenly lost his desire for coffee and certainly didn't feel like chitchat. His conversation with Lee was yet another reminder of the things he had hoped to forget. At least for the morning.

But just as he was about to leave, his mother called out to him, hurrying to his side. "Vic. There you are. I've been looking for you." She rested her hand on the table as she caught her breath.

"You okay?" Vic asked, suddenly concerned.

"Just had to rush to catch you." She gave

him a quick smile, her frizzy graying hair catching the light coming in from the large floor-to-ceiling windows from one wall of the room. Her glasses sat askew on her nose. Her shirt was bunched up over the belt she wore and her ruffled skirt, a throwback to the 80s, hung crooked.

His dear mother always said she didn't care how she looked and it showed.

"We've got company coming over for lunch," she said, moving her hand to indicate the woman who now joined them.

Vic's heart did a double flip as he took in Lauren's restrained elegance. Fitted brown dress, white belt, shoes and purse, and a fancy necklace that sparkled in the overhead lights. She wore her hair loose, but it was smooth and silky, and as she tipped her head toward him it slipped away from her face.

His mother's words finally registered. "Company?"

His mother gestured to Lauren. "Yes. I was talking to Keith's girl and said she should come over for lunch. She tried to object, but I wouldn't take no for an answer. I know her sister Jodie is gone to Bozeman this weekend and she doesn't know anybody here anymore, so I told her she simply had to come. No excuses."

"I'm sorry," Lauren apologized. "If it doesn't work out—"

"Nonsense," his mother said, patting her on the shoulder. "Nothing to work out. Dean's sulking at home and I could use some female company and we have lots of food. Besides, I promised her some daylilies and peony roots."

Vic could tell that Lauren was trying to find a polite way to get out of the invitation, though he knew it was futile. Once his mother set her mind to something, she would not let go. And of late she'd been complaining about being lonely. He guessed Lauren had mentioned her desire to clean up the flower beds on the Circle M and his plant-loving mother had probably jumped at the chance to talk botany with another woman.

"Just come for a while," he encouraged her. "It's got to be lonely sitting in that house by yourself. Unless you need to plant your flowers," he teased.

She smiled, which only served to make her more attractive.

"No. I'm letting them harden off before I put them in the ground."

"You won't need to do that," his mother said. "It's late enough that you could put them directly in. But we can talk more about that at home. You can follow us to our place. Just in case you don't know the way." Before anyone could make even the slightest objection, his mother bustled off again.

It was on the tip of Vic's tongue to let Lauren know that she didn't have to accept his mother's invitation, but he stopped himself. It might not hurt his cause if Lauren could meet Dean again. Put a face to the reason he needed to buy the ranch.

Chapter Five

"So what kind of work do you do?" Vic's mother pushed her empty plate aside and seemed more than happy to put off cleaning up until later. She tucked her curly hair back from her face and clamped it down with a hair clip that had been threatening to fall out.

Based on how casual Mrs. Moore seemed about her clothing choices, Lauren had suspected her home would be a reflection of that. But driving up to the two-story brick-and-sandstone home, Lauren shifted mental gears. The house was a beautiful mix of old and new. A wild array of flowering shrubs, perennials and potted plants softened the front of the house. Yet it didn't look stilted or planned.

The inside of the house was equally surprising. The appliances were basic white, but the wooden cupboards were an updated dark walnut with brushed aluminum hardware. The floor was a gray laminate and the dining room table and chairs were an elegant mix of wood and stainless steel.

Clearly Mrs. Moore cared more about her home than she did about how she looked. Lauren admired the woman, knowing that she herself had spent far too much of her own life worrying about the correct image she needed to project.

"I work as an accountant," Lauren said, wiping her mouth with a cloth napkin.

"My goodness. Numbers." Mrs. Moore fluttered her hands. "Benny always said I was horrible with numbers and he was right. Balancing the checkbook to me meant being able to carry it and my groceries without dropping either."

Lauren giggled, surprised at how comfortable she felt around the older woman.

"Good thing you don't need to balance the checkbook anymore," Vic chimed in, smiling at his mother. "Dean takes care of everything online," he said to Lauren.

"One of the few things I can do," Dean said, a grumpy note in his voice. He wore a plaid shirt that had seen better days, faded blue jeans with holes in the knees, a large leg brace and a sullen attitude.

The stubble on his handsome face didn't soften the hardened look he seemed to have adopted. Lauren remembered another Dean. Cocky. Self-assured.

This young man seemed to have lost that part of his persona.

"But you have a good job for now until you are able to work on the ranch again," his mother said with a smile for her youngest son.

"What do you do now, Dean?" Lauren asked, trying to draw the taciturn young man into the conversation. She remembered Dean well from the summers she'd spent here. He'd been a wild young man who lived a rough life. He'd also had a huge crush on Erin. But both Jodie and Lauren had warned her away from him. Thankfully she'd listened. Dean had hung out with David Fortier and Mitch Albon, both young men of questionable reputation. Now David was dead and Mitch was in prison. Dean, it seemed, had escaped that. Probably thanks to his stable family life.

"I work part-time as a finishing carpenter for Jan Peter. He's a big time contractor out here. But I guess I'll need to talk to him about full-time work."

Lauren shot Vic a puzzled look. "I thought you ranched with Vic." Hadn't Vic told her that he had figured on buying the Circle M for his brother?

"If you want to call what I do ranching." He released a bitter laugh. "And thanks to you, my life is going in a different direction."

"Dean. That's enough," Vic said. "Lauren is our guest."

Lauren's heart shifted as Dean's anger washed over her. Ranching wasn't in his future because she was selling the Circle M ranch.

She shouldn't have come.

Dean sighed, then turned to Lauren. "I'm sorry. I'm just in a lot of pain right now. That was out of line." Dean pushed his chair away from the table and grabbed a crutch. "I gotta go lie down."

He limped off, the thump of his crutch echoing in the silence.

Mrs. Moore watched him go, and Lauren saw the sorrow on her face. Poor woman, dealing with so many losses in one year.

"I'm so sorry," Mrs. Moore said. "But please, don't take it personally. He's been bitter since the accident and then his father's death." Her voice wobbled and Lauren felt a rush of sympathy for her.

"I understand," she said, reaching across the table to cover her hand in sympathy. "I have no doubt this has been a difficult time. For you, too."

Mrs. Moore gave her a grateful smile. "You're a sweetheart. It has been hard, but God has given us the strength to deal with it all. I don't know what I would do without knowing that He's watching over us." Mrs. Moore squeezed Lauren's hand. "I'm sure you feel the same way. What with your father's death and all. You girls had your own struggles, I know."

Lauren held her gaze, feeling a fraud by taking her concern, yet surprised at the affection she felt for this caring woman. Her own mother had been distant, dealing with her own sorrows. Yet here was this woman, a stranger to Lauren, feeling sorry for her.

"My faith has helped me through many of life's trials" was all she could say, unwilling to let go of Mrs. Moore's hand. It had been so long since someone other than her sisters, whom she seldom saw, had shown her affection. Had touched her like this. It warmed her soul.

Mrs. Moore gave her hands another squeeze, then sat back. "So tell me more about your work. You must be smart as all get-out if you work as an accountant."

Not smart enough to stay employed, Lauren

thought with a too-familiar twinge of anger at her previous boss.

"I know how to work with numbers" was all Lauren could say.

"Will you be doing that here? In Saddlebank?" Mrs. Moore asked.

"No. I won't." Lauren couldn't help a quick glance Vic's way. She guessed from his mother's surprise at Dean's comment that Mrs. Moore didn't know of her plans.

"So you'll be supervising Vic's leasing the ranch?" Mrs. Moore asked.

"I can't make any decisions until I've stayed at the ranch for two months," she said, keeping things vague. No reason to bring up the topic of her selling the ranch.

"Saddlebank is a good place to raise a family," Mrs. Moore said with a melancholy smile. "Benny, my late husband, and I, were so thankful to be able to raise our boys here. I'm sure you would find the same if you gave it a chance. Being married and raising children is a wonderful thing." Mrs. Moore gave her an encouraging look and Lauren felt once again the twinge of sorrow that Harvey's breakup had caused her. The humiliation and the loss.

"Not everyone needs to find fulfillment in

that," Vic said. "That was your choice and it worked for you."

"But it could work for you, too," Mrs. Moore said. The touch of sorrow in her voice made Lauren realize that Mrs. Moore's marriage comment was aimed at her son, not her. "That Tiffany girl was no good for either you or Dean. You were right not to go chasing after her."

Lauren saw Vic's lips thin and guessed his mother had brought up a painful topic. While part of her was curious, she knew it was none of her business.

"I understand you also had Finn Hicks living in your home awhile?" Lauren asked, steering the conversation to a safer topic. "Jodie told me that he moved in with you and your family when he was in his teens."

Vic's wry smile told her that he knew exactly what she was up to and that he was thankful for it.

"Yes. We did," Mrs. Moore said, latching on to the subject. "That poor boy's father had died and his mother was all over creation and he needed a home. But now he's got his own place, and he and Jodie are getting married. Things work out the way they're supposed to. And what about you? Any young man in your life?"

Mrs. Moore seemed determined to come back to marriage as a topic.

"No. No young man."

"Well, now, that's too bad." Mrs. Moore leaned her elbow on the table, looking past Lauren to the wall behind her, where she remembered seeing a series of framed pictures. "Having someone to share your life with is special. Benny was my life. My anchor." She paused and Lauren thought she might cry. According to Drake, her lawyer, it had only been about four months since Mrs. Moore's husband, Vic's father, passed away.

Then Mrs. Moore slapped her hands on the table and stood, as if putting her sorrow behind her.

"I need to lie down for a nap," she said, glancing from Lauren to Vic. "And I don't want to listen to the clatter of dishes, so I want you two to just leave them alone. Vic, why don't you take Lauren out and show her where the lilies are? The peonies are over by the garage and there's also some monkshood she's welcome to take."

"I don't think I'll need that much—" Lauren started to object.

"There's pots in the potting shed," Mrs. Moore continued, waving off Lauren's comment. "And you can use the narrow shovel to dig them up and the wagon to cart them around. You'll have to put them in your truck to bring them to her place. If you need help planting them, Lauren, let me know. And don't even think about doing the dishes."

Before either Lauren or Vic could say anything, she swept out of the kitchen and down the hall.

"Well, I guess I got my work cut out for me this afternoon," Vic said getting to his feet.

"You don't have to do this," Lauren demurred. "I feel kind of silly coming here and taking plants from your mother. Like she said, it's not the right time of the year anyway."

"I wouldn't fuss about that. My mother loves nothing more than to share the wealth of her garden and to know that the legacy of her mother lives on."

"Legacy?" she asked as she followed Vic out of the house.

"My mom got most of the plants in the yard from her mother, who, apparently, got them from hers. She claims to have single-handedly brought rare Marcher daylilies to Saddlebank County."

"Never heard of them," Lauren admitted as she headed out the back door of the house and through a pair of patio doors onto a deck.

And as she did, she came to a sudden stop,

staring at the garden in front of her. Shrubs and trees edged two acres of verdant green lawn. They, in turn, were framed by bricked-in flower beds holding flowers of varying heights and color. An old bicycle covered in ivy rested among two-foot-high delphiniums, lilies, monkshood, bleeding heart, daisies, marigolds and pansies in another flower bed opposite.

In the shade of a white pergola, tubs with geraniums, million bells, lobelia and sweet potato vine nestled against wicker chairs. A small creek bisected the garden, flowing under an arched bridge that held pots of brightly colored aspermums.

It was like a sheltered oasis. An English estate garden transplanted to Montana. She could hardly take it all in.

"Impressive, isn't it," Vic said, standing with his hands on his hips as he surveyed the garden. "Took Mom about fifteen years, a lot of nagging and sweat equity from me, Dean and my dad to get it to this."

"It's amazing." Beyond the bridge Lauren saw a gazebo also hung with more pots. "How does she keep this all up?"

"It's what she does. And it's been good for her this spring. It's kept her busy after Dad died. Gave her a focus."

Vic wandered down the bricked path and over the bridge. Lauren followed him, but she felt the garden calling her to sit. Rest. Contemplate the beauty around her.

But Vic was a man with a mission, so she followed him past the gazebo, then through an opening in the row of trees at the far end of the garden. Once past the trees, the land opened up and she saw fenced pasture and fields rolling toward the mountains that cradled the basin.

Vic kept walking, following a pole fence that meandered toward a small garage. "Just wait here. I'll get the quad and trailer," he said as he pulled open the large double doors.

Lauren stayed where she was as she heard a small engine start up. Vic drove a small ATV out of the shop, pulling a trailer behind him.

"I'll just get a shovel and we're good to go," he said, disappearing inside again.

He came out with only one shovel.

"We'll need two," she said.

"I'll do the digging," Vic said as he tossed the shovel into the large, open trailer. "You can tell me what you want."

"Nonsense," Lauren said. "I can help."

"In that dress?"

"It's fine. Plus, I'm wearing flats."

"They're white."

"And washable."

Vic gave her another quick look and she felt suddenly self-conscious. She had chosen her clothes carefully. Though she didn't want to examine why, she had hoped, on one level, that Vic would be at church. But compared to his casual mother, she now felt like a vain fashion model.

She pushed past him, stepping into the dim interior. When her eyes adjusted she spied an entire array of gardening tools hanging neatly on one wall. She grabbed a shovel, stepped outside and gave him a look that dared him to say anything.

"Okay. I'll just get some pots and we can go," he said. He disappeared inside again and came out with a huge stack of empty pots nested inside each other.

She couldn't imagine that she'd take that many plants.

"So where next?" she asked.

"Hop on and we'll head over there."

Lauren looked from the seat of the ATV to Vic now swinging his leg over the seat and settling onto it. She doubted she would fit behind him. And how was she supposed to get on in her narrow skirt?

"You'll have to ride sidesaddle behind me," Vic said with a grin.

"I can walk," she said.

"Be easier just to ride. You're not scared of me, are you?"

He said it with a teasing tone, but at the same time Lauren heard an underlying challenge.

She stepped on the footrest of the quad and dropped into the seat behind Vic.

But she had moved too quickly and became unbalanced and the only way to recover was to grab Vic's shoulder.

His very large, muscular shoulder.

Vic took off and as she teetered on her precarious seat, wishing once again that she'd gone with her first choice of slacks and a blazer. But she'd wanted to look feminine this morning. Feminine and in charge. So she put on the dress that Amy called her power dress. The one she wore when she wanted to make an impression on clients.

Only she doubted it made any impression on Vic.

"I'm driving around to the side of the house," Vic said over the noise of the engine. "But we need to go through the fields first to get to the road leading there. Just in case you think I'm kidnapping you."

She laughed. "The quad and trailer were my

first clue that you aren't," she returned. "Plus I could probably run faster than this machine."

"Oh, don't underestimate how fast this thing can go," Vic called back. "I've had it up to forty miles an hour."

"No, thanks," she said with a laugh.

"Then you'd really have to hang on," he said, shooting her a quick backward glance.

Lauren held his eyes a moment, then looked away, too easily imagining herself clinging to his broad back. The thought held an appeal that spoke to the loneliness of the past year.

You don't need a man, remember? You have your own plans and you need to stick with them.

But even as she repeated the mantra, it rang hollow.

Vic drove through an opening in a row of cottonwoods and shrubs, coming, as promised, to the side of the house. They came upon another large flower garden hidden from the driveway by more cottonwoods.

"This is what my mom calls her free-range garden," Vic said as he stopped and turned off the quad. "You can pick whatever you want from here."

This garden looked wilder, but at the same time Lauren could tell that it was cared for and nurtured.

The ground was still wet from the rain on Saturday and she was thankful she hadn't worn heels that would have sunk into the ground.

She stopped by a group of daylilies, the pink and purple blossoms waving in the light breeze.

"How many of these do you want?"

All of them, Lauren wanted to say as she took in the swath of color. It made her heart happy to see the glorious blooms and she bent down to have a closer look at one of the delicate flowers. "I've never seen one like this."

"That's the Marcher lily I was telling you about. Extremely rare, according to my mother."

"If there's enough to spare, I'd love one." She knew exactly where to plant it. The purple and pink of the lily would go well with the red geraniums she had chosen to plant in the flower bed on the side of the house.

"Your wish is my command," he said, slipping on his gloves and grabbing the shovel. With one quick push of his booted foot on the shovel, he cut into the ground around the plant she had indicated. She grabbed her shovel as well and helped to cut through the dirt, but she couldn't push down as far as Vic could. Even so, she kept going, determined to do her part.

A few moments later Vic was tipping a large clump of sod and plant over. Lauren grabbed a large pot and dragged it over, frustrated with the restriction of her narrow skirt.

With a twist of the shovel Vic lifted the mass of dirt and dropped it neatly into the pot. Lauren bent over to pick it up and with a heave, managed to get it into the wagon. She got dirt all over her dress, but she didn't care.

"You'll have to dig a big hole for that one," Vic warned.

"I'll be wearing more suitable gardening clothes when I do that," Lauren said, brushing at the dirt on her dress.

"Any other color you want?"

Lauren bit her lip, trying to decide.

"You know what, why don't you take one of each?" he said. "Get a bunch of pots and we can get working."

"I don't think I can take that many."

"I told you, my mom wants you to have them."

"But—"

Then to her surprise Vic pulled off his gloves and touched her lips as if to silence her. It was the merest whisper of a touch, but she felt as if her mouth had been branded. As if the air had been vacuumed out of her body.

Vic's eyes held hers and she saw confusion

in their dark depths. As if he didn't know himself what he had just done.

She swallowed and looked away. "I guess... I could find space..."

"Sorry about that," he said. "It's a silly habit. I do it to my mom when she...when she talks too much."

"It's okay," she said, determined to sound casual but at the same time unable to stop her eyes from seeking his again.

But he frowned at the plants as if his mind was already figuring out how to do this as he yanked his gloves on again.

Twenty minutes and sixteen pots later, the trailer was full of a delightful variety of plants in a rainbow of colors.

She wanted to go home right away and plant them all. She didn't know if she had space for that many plants, but Vic seemed determined to capitalize on his mother's generous offer.

Why bother planting them all? You won't even be around to enjoy them.

Lauren stilled the pernicious voice. Planting them gave her something enjoyable to do to fill her time.

"You look happy," Vic said as he lugged the last pot of peonies onto the trailer.

"I'm excited to get them in the ground."

Vic pulled a hankie out of his pocket and wiped off his face. "I know you're wanting to make the place look nice but truthfully, I can't think of any rancher I know that bought a ranch because it had peonies and lilies."

She heard the teasing tone in his voice, but at the same time her thoughts shifted to Dean—the true reason Vic wanted to buy her father's place.

"It gives me something to do."

"I can appreciate that," Vic said. He picked up his shovel and set it on the trailer. "Speaking of the sale, I'll be coming by tomorrow to finish up the haying. It should be dry after today. But it won't take me all day. I was hoping to go through the rest of your father's papers we didn't get to the last time I was there."

She looked into his eyes and her breath stilled, her heart slowed and everything around them faded away. It was just her and Vic in this idyllic setting.

He's getting too close. You have to be careful. Don't you ever learn?

And yet, she couldn't help a flicker of sympathy at his dilemma. Seeing Dean struggle, hearing his bitterness, was a tangible reminder to her of why Vic wanted to buy the ranch.

"I'm sorry that my dad didn't take better care of you and your brother," she said.

"I am, too." He pulled in a breath, then turned away. "I can take you home as soon as I load these up."

"No. That would be inhospitable," Lauren said, setting her shovel on the trailer. "In spite of what your mom said, I would like to go in and at least clean up if your mom or Dean aren't awake yet."

"Dean most likely didn't go to bed. I'm guessing he's out in the barn. Reading or resting his leg."

"I heard he injured it in a rodeo accident. How did that happen?" Jodie had made a brief mention of it but hadn't said how.

"Took a bad spill off a saddle bronc." He turned away. "Let's load up these plants."

His words were abrupt, and as he grabbed a few of the pots and brought them to his truck, Lauren sensed there was more to the story.

And for some reason she wanted to know what it was.

Vic pulled into the yard and parked by his brother's truck. Thankfully Dean was still home. He had delivered Lauren's plants as he'd promised his mother, but the entire time he was gone he had wondered if Dean would take off.

He had been in a lousy mood all morning

and Vic suspected seeing Lauren and what she represented probably hadn't helped.

After the accident Dean had changed. Had become a bit more settled. And when he started working for Jan he starting talking seriously about working together with Vic and ranching together.

Then Lauren had come with her plans that changed everything.

He let his thoughts drift to her, confused at his changing reactions.

It had been easy to be with her this afternoon. Picking out plants. Laughing about how many she wanted and how he had to keep reassuring her that it didn't matter how many she took.

Then he'd touched her.

Vic winced at the memory. He still wasn't sure what had gotten into him, only that his gesture had been automatic. Instinctive.

At least she hadn't jerked away.

And don't read more into that, he reminded himself as he shoved the door of the truck open and clambered out, striding to the house.

After he and Lauren had finished digging up the plants, they had come inside, only to discover that his mother was still sleeping. Lauren insisted that they clean up as much as they could. But still his mother didn't wake. So they left.

His mother was up when he came into the kitchen, sitting at the table with a cup of tea and a gardening magazine. "So did you find enough plants?" she asked.

"More than enough. I think she'll be busy the next few days planting them all." He dropped into a chair across from her. "You have a good nap?"

"Yes, I did."

"Lauren wanted me to make sure to pass on her thanks once again. She felt bad that you weren't up when she came back into the house."

"I was sorry, too, but I was so exhausted. I haven't been sleeping right."

"Why did you invite her to come if you were so tired?" Vic asked.

"I was just being hospitable." His mother took a sip of her tea and flipped a page in the magazine. But Vic caught a hint of a smile and suspected that his mother was up to something else.

"She seems like a nice girl," she continued. "Not at all what I expected, considering how Keith used to complain about her."

"Keith complained a lot the last few years," Vic said as he took a cookie from the plate sitting on the table. It was hard not to sound churlish. Lauren's question about Dean's accident made him feel guiltier about what happened. And more determined to make it right.

"She's a lovely person. And attractive. I understand that she's single. Keith made some comment about her being left at the altar. He had planned to go to North Carolina for her wedding, then suddenly it got canceled."

As she spoke, the memory came back to him—Keith complaining about the change in plans, as if his daughter's canceled wedding was all about him. Now that he'd met Lauren, that moment took on a deeper meaning. While he had hoped seeing Dean would make her realize what was at stake, spending time with her made him aware of what she had lost, as well.

He didn't want to feel sorry for her. She had been on his mind too much already the past few days. He had to keep his mind on what he needed to do.

Keep his focus on his brother and his needs.

Chapter Six

Lauren sat back on her haunches, unable to stop smiling at the flower garden that was slowly rising from the tangle of weeds. Jodie was coming home this afternoon and Lauren was excited to show her the transformation.

The bare spaces left when she pulled out the endless weeds were now filled with a mixture of the flowers Mrs. Moore had given her and those she had purchased at the greenhouse the other day.

Though she knew cutting the blooms off would help establish the plant's root system, she couldn't. They looked so friendly and cheerful, adding a bright and pleasant note to the front of the house.

They made it look more like a home.

The thought drifted in her mind, and for

a small moment she let it settle, then with a shake of her head dislodged it.

It's just the ranch.

She brushed the dirt off her pants and pushed herself to her feet, wiping her forehead with the back of her hand. The day had started out so fresh and clear, but now the heat of the afternoon sun beat down on her.

In the distance she saw Vic making his rounds with the tractor and baler. The field was large and he'd appear for a while, then as he moved farther on, disappear. He'd been here since midmorning, and from what she could see he was only half-done.

The tractor was an older one and every window was wide-open. If she was hot working out in the open, he must be cooking inside that tractor.

She set the empty pots back on the wheelbarrow, lifted it up and wheeled it across the yard to where Vic's truck was parked. In the bed of his truck sat the empty tubs the plants from his mother had come in.

Sweat trickled down her back and her hands, inside her leather gloves, were slick. Thank goodness she had worn a hat or she might have to worry about sunstroke.

Once again her eyes moved to where Vic

worked. The tractor was stopped, the baler whining.

He must be winding the twine around the bale, she thought, remembering the sound from when her father had done the same work.

Another memory came to her—walking across the prickly hay field with Erin, bringing a container of lemonade to their father while he was working.

You should do that for Vic.

She shook off that thought. He had probably brought his own drink.

But it would be warm and gross by now. It would be a kind and neighborly thing to do.

Part of her knew that, but another part of her—the part that could still feel the touch of his finger on her lips, see the intensity of his expression—held back. Seeing Vic with his mother and brother, working alongside him digging plants, talking to him in church, had all added to a growing attraction.

She knew she couldn't get distracted. She had to keep her focus.

He dug up all those plants for you—surely you can do something kind for him.

She looked up at the cloudless sky, then at her watch. He would be out there for at least another couple of hours.

Before she could talk herself out of it, she strode to the house and went directly to the pantry, hoping the large canister of lemonade crystals her father always had on hand was still there.

She was in luck—she found not one but two containers. She pulled one down and brought it to the kitchen. It took her a few more minutes to find the insulated drink container they often used. When she pulled it out from the pantry, she felt a surprising touch of nostalgia, remembering bringing their father lemonade. How grateful he'd been.

She dropped ice into the container, added the lemonade crystals and poured the water in. She found a plastic bag, added some oatmeal-raisin cookies she had baked yesterday, grabbed two plastic cups, and a few minutes later was walking down the field. The increasing roar of the tractor told her that it was coming closer. She had timed it just right.

Shielding her eyes, she saw Vic in the cab, and as he came closer, she noticed him frowning.

Probably figured she had one more piece of bad news to deliver.

He slowed down as she approached and came to a stop right beside her.

She held up the container with lemonade and the bag of cookies.

"Thought you might want a break," she called out over the roar of the tractor.

His grin was a white flash on his dusty face. He shut the tractor off and climbed out.

"That sounds amazing," he said pulling his ever-present hankie out of his pocket. "I forgot to take extra water along today. I'm kind of parched." He wiped his face as best he could, then shoved the hankie back in his pocket. "Are you going to join me? Unless you're too busy making the flower garden magazine-worthy."

"It will never be anything like your mother's place," she said with a quick laugh. "And yes, I'll join you."

"I don't think any place will be or should be like my mother's," Vic returned, taking the container from her. "We can sit in the shade of the tractor. Unless the grass will be too scratchy for you."

"I may be from the city, but I'm about one-sixth country," she said with a challenge in her voice.

"Only one-sixth?"

"The two months of the year I spent here."

"Plus the time you lived here."

"Less the time I didn't."

"I should know better than to argue numbers with an accountant."

She chuckled as she found a place to sit.

He waited until she got herself settled on the ground before he sat down himself. She handed him a cup and he poured them both some lemonade. Then she held out the bag and he took a cookie from it. He took a long drink and then released a contented sigh. "That's amazing. Thanks so much," he said as he started munching on the cookie.

"You're welcome. I used to do this for my father."

"Ah. Country girl at heart."

"A bit."

"Did you ever ride when you were out here?"

"A bit."

He laughed at that. "If you ever feel the desire to go riding, the horses that Jodie has here are safe to ride. Finn has been working with them."

"So I heard. Jodie assured me I could take them out anytime I wanted."

"Have you?"

"I went out on my own on Saturday night," she returned, lifting her chin in a small gesture of defiance. "It was fun."

"I'd like to have seen that," he said. "Where did you go?"

"Just down the road to a trail leading to the river. Nothing dramatic."

"Those are usually the best rides," he said. He flashed her another grin and she returned it with one of her own, enjoying the easy give-and-take with this man. He was comfortable to be around.

She pulled her legs up to her chest, wrapping her arms around them as she took in the silence surrounding them. Far off she heard the lowing of the cows from the pasture across the road. The sound was an idyllic counterpoint to the chirping of sparrows and the croak of frogs from a creek splashing through the cottonwoods.

A few lazy flies buzzed around and Lauren released a long, slow sigh.

"You sound like you're decompressing," Vic said, pushing his cowboy hat farther back on his head.

"I feel like I am." She spoke softly as if afraid to disturb the moment. "I keep forgetting how quiet it is out here. How isolated."

"It's not that isolated. My ranch is down the road in one direction, the Bannister ranch in the other."

"I know, but in Chicago and New York we live stacked on top of each other, side by side. It's never quiet. Never."

She stopped, listening again, a smile lingering on her lips. A gentle calm and a desire to stay right where she was suffused her.

"I don't think I could handle that," Vic said, pouring some more lemonade for himself. He held the jug out to Lauren, but she declined a refill.

"I don't think you could, either," Lauren said, glancing over at Vic. She tried to picture him strolling down a city sidewalk, past office towers, in that rolling gait of his. The walk of a cowboy. It didn't jell.

"But you're used to it?"

"Got used to it," she admitted. "Don't forget, I've been living in large towns and cities ever since we left here."

A breeze started up just as she reached for the lemonade container to screw the lid down. Her hair was blown in her face, sticking to her lipstick, and she tried to shake it away but it wouldn't move.

She felt rough fingers on her face, tucking the strands of hair behind her ear.

It was a light touch. An innocent gesture that probably meant nothing to Vic, but it sent a thrill of awareness sparking down her neck.

She couldn't help how her head turned toward him as he lowered his hand. She felt a sense of waiting. Expectation.

Then his phone beeped an incoming text and Lauren pulled herself back to reality. Vic glanced at his phone but chose to ignore it. He set it down on the ground between them.

"Don't forget to pick that up again," she said, pleased that her voice didn't sound as shaky as she felt.

"I won't. I don't go anywhere without my phone. My mom says it's unhealthy."

"It's unhealthy for me if I forget it."

"Why?"

"I get all jittery thinking I might miss some important call. Back in the city we call it FOMO—fear of missing out."

He chuckled. "I'm guessing you have your phone with you now?"

"Back pocket."

He smiled as he took another cookie, and she was thankful for the easy give-and-take between them. Just two people spending time together. Nothing more.

"You make these?" Vic asked.

"The only kind I know how to make, much to my grandmother's disappointment. She always said oatmeal-raisin cookies were the reason she has trust issues."

Vic's frown told her he didn't get the old family joke.

"She always thought they were chocolate

chips and got disappointed. She never liked raisins. In anything."

"And yet you continued to make cookies with raisins?"

"Because I like them and it was the only recipe that turned out well for me," she returned, taking another drink of her own chilled lemonade. "Erin was the one who liked baking every kind of cookie and cake she found on the internet and in any cookbook my aunt had lying around."

"Jodie much of a baker?"

"No. She was the entertainer of the family."

"Youngest child," he said, taking another cookie out of the bag.

"You know of what you speak?"

"Dean's the same way. Or used to be."

"How is he doing today?"

"Better. He's helping Jan today, so that helps. Lets him feel useful."

Her thoughts shifted to the conversation they had at his mother's place. The abrupt way he had turned away from her when she brought up Dean's accident. She knew she should leave it alone, but her curiosity got the better of her.

"So how exactly did he get hurt?"

"He got dumped off a saddle bronc."

"And that's how he broke his leg?"

"No. That happened when he got tangled up in the gate he fell on."

Lauren winced. And couldn't help notice the harshness in Vic's voice. There was more to it than this.

"Has he been riding saddle broncs long?"

"Since he was a little kid." Vic raised one leg and rested his forearm on his knee as he stared off, as if returning to that moment. "It wasn't lack of experience that caused the accident. I should've paid attention."

His comment puzzled her. "What do you mean *you* should've paid attention?"

Vic's face grew hard and his eyes narrowed. In the silence that followed, she wondered if he was going to say anything at all.

"I was riding pickup that evening," he said, his voice quiet. "I was supposed to be watching. I was supposed to grab him if he was in trouble. I didn't notice—"

He stopped, abruptly finished off the last of his lemonade and set the cup aside.

"So you think it's your fault that he got hurt?"

"I don't *think* it is, I *know* it is." Vic sounded angry.

Slowly things fell into place.

"You want the ranch for Dean because of what happened," she said.

Vic's eyes latched on to hers and Lauren wondered if she had pushed him too hard, said too much.

But as he held her gaze, his shoulders seem to slump and he leaned back against the tractor tire. He moved his hand over his chin, as if debating what to say next. "No secret I want the ranch for Dean. I told you that from the beginning."

"No. But I didn't know it was because you felt guilty. About what happened to Dean."

"I don't feel—" He stopped himself, blew out a breath and released a harsh laugh. "You're the first person that seems to have put all that together."

"Not the first. You have, too. And I wonder if Dean has."

"Doesn't matter. I have to do this. I have to try," he amended. "And I know it won't work for you if I find that agreement, but I still need to try."

She understood completely, recognizing the burden of every firstborn child. The need to take care of everyone, to take on the responsibility of everyone. Once again doubts assailed her.

Stop overthinking this. For once put yourself first. It's what you want, what you need.

The little mental lecture centered her. But

at the same time she was sorry the topic of Dean had come up. For a few moments she'd felt a connection with Vic. For a few moments she'd shared ordinary conversation with an appealing man. It was nice.

Dangerous, but still nice.

Then her phone rang and all hope of any normal conversation with Vic fled.

It was Alex Rossiter.

Vic finished off the last of his cookie as he tried not to listen to Lauren's phone conversation. He knew she was talking to her buyer.

"I know you told me you were coming tomorrow," she said, her voice sounding strained. "But I forgot to make plans." She nodded as Vic faintly heard the chatter of a male voice.

The buyer.

The man with all the money.

Then she said goodbye and slipped the phone into her back pocket again.

"So what does he want?" Vic asked, wiping the remnants of cookie crumbs off his pants.

"He asked me last week if he could come tomorrow." She scratched her chin with her forefinger as if thinking. "He wants me to show him around the ranch, but…"

"You don't know that much about it," he

finished for her, remembering the phone call she got when he brought her to town.

"I know something, but I haven't been here for over ten years. And I thought—"

"You want me to show him around."

She looked over at him, her eyes pleading. "I would feel better if someone who knew the ranch could talk to him about it."

He exhaled, shoving his hair back from his face in a gesture of frustration. What irony. Escorting the future buyer over the ranch he had counted on buying himself.

Though he hoped to go through more of the papers in Keith's office tomorrow, he was starting to see the futility of it all. All they had found so far was an old lease agreement Keith had drawn up with Rusty Granger— frustrating that he had protected Rusty's interests but not his—and a host of grocery lists and to-do lists, but that was about it.

He doubted that a further search of the office would yield anything more. And yet he knew he had to give it one more try.

"I know it's a lot to ask and I'm sorry—"

"I'll do it," he said as he got to his feet.

She stood as well, looking sheepish. "Thanks. I appreciate it."

"What time is he coming?"

"About noonish tomorrow. Does that work?"

"I'll be done haying today, provided I don't get any more distractions." In spite of his irritation with the situation, he couldn't help smiling at her. He appreciated the lemonade and cookies, and the fact that she had taken the time to think about him.

"I won't bug you anymore," she said, returning his smile.

"Bringing lemonade and homemade cookies hardly constitutes bugging." He looked over at her and to his surprise she didn't turn away. As their eyes locked, he felt an age-old emotion rise up in him. The beginnings of appeal and connection. The hesitant looks. The careful dance between a man and a woman signaling a shift toward attraction.

Be careful. This one isn't for you. She's not sticking around. She created a host of problems for you.

But in spite of the very wise and practical voice warning him, he kept his eyes on Lauren and she on him.

He wanted to touch her face, brush his fingers over her flushed cheek. The impulse was so strong, he felt his hand rising.

Then she turned away—the moment was gone—and he clenched his fist, frustrated with how she was insinuating herself into his life. Yesterday, after he came back from delivering her plants at the ranch, he'd found his thoughts returning to her again and again.

Reliving that moment when he had touched her.

He gave himself a shake, then bent to pick up his phone.

He frowned when he saw two identical black phones lying in the cut hay, neither of them with covers.

"Which one of these is yours?" he asked, picking them both up.

She looked as puzzled as he was, then took one. "I think it's this one," she said, hitting the home button.

A picture of his mother and Dean flashed on the screen and she handed it over to him. "Sorry. I didn't mean to intrude."

"That's okay," he said, handing her the other phone. "It was a perfectly innocuous picture."

She shoved her phone in her back pocket and gave him a wistful smile. "It's sweet."

Somehow the compliment fell awkwardly between them.

Sweet.

"So I can tell Alex to come tomorrow?" she asked.

"Yeah. Sure." Vic dropped his phone in his shirt pocket. "Tell him two is probably best.

I should be done by then." Then he climbed back in the tractor.

Lauren was already walking away, carrying the lemonade container in one hand and the bag with the cookies and the cups in the other. He started up the tractor, backed up and lined himself up with the swath of hay and moved ahead.

But before he started moving, he glanced over at Lauren again.

Only to see her looking at him. She lifted her hand holding the bag, waggled her fingers at him, turned and walked away.

What was that about?

You're being all high school. Don't read too much into that.

And yet, as he started working, that simple gesture stayed with him.

As did her smile.

Chapter Seven

"We generally put the cows out on these pastures first thing in the spring," Vic was saying as he walked with Alex Rossiter past the fenced fields across the road from the ranch house. The cows in the pasture were just brown and black dots farther back, closer to the hills. "Then, as the snow retreats on the mountains and the grass starts growing farther up, we move them to the higher pastures."

Lauren followed a few steps behind, feeling useless but at the same time thankful Vic had agreed to this. She knew that her father moved the cows partway through the summer. She and her sisters had participated in a pasture move years ago.

It had been one of those idyllic days. Sunlight poured from blue sky devoid of clouds.

A faint breeze kept bugs at bay and the rhythmic plod of the horses they rode had lulled the McCauley sisters and their father into a good mood.

The memory made her smile.

But it wasn't the kind of information you could pass on to a prospective buyer.

"How many head can you run?" Alex was asking, punching something into his phone, which never left his hand.

"Two hundred in this pasture with proper pasture management."

"Management as in?"

"Rotation. Moving them around more frequently."

"Sure. Whatever," Alex muttered as his fingers flew over the screen's keyboard.

The conversation drifted past Lauren, again somewhat familiar but not information she knew.

She sensed an edge of tension to Vic's voice. He most likely wasn't the most objective guide, she realized, but he was the one who knew the place the best.

"How long has this ranch been operating?" Alex asked, turning to Lauren. "You're the owner, after all—you should know that."

He winked at her. The last time she met Alex Rossiter, it was at her office. He had worn an open-necked shirt, a gold chain, a blazer and blue jeans that were artfully faded and distressed. And expensive. As were his John Lobb tasseled loafers.

Today he had gone with the more down-home cowboy look. Plaid shirt, plain blue jeans, cowboy boots so new they still shone, and topping it all off, a straw cowboy hat, crisp and gleaming.

Then there was Vic, with his twill shirt rolled up at the sleeves, stained leather gloves shoved in the back pockets of blue jeans faded at the knees and ragged at the hem, worn over scuffed cowboy boots. His hat was weathered and sat easily on his head, almost an extension of himself. Authentic. Man of the land.

He looked rooted. Grounded.

Alex was a nice guy, a pleasant man, in fact, but compared to Vic he seemed insubstantial.

His money wasn't. And she needed every penny of it.

"The ownership of this ranch goes back many generations," Lauren said. She leaned against a fence post, dredging up the history lessons her father gave them whenever he thought they needed reminders of their past. "My father inherited it from his father, whose wife was related to the Bannister family of

Refuge Ranch, which is farther up the valley. Before that it's a tangle of Bannister and McCauley ownership. I think I ran across a family tree going through my father's papers. I can show it to you if you're interested."

Alex waved off the offer. "No. I was just making conversation."

His comment was throwaway, but she couldn't shed it that easily as her gaze traveled over the fields she had ridden on as a young girl, the fields her father and his father and grandfather had owned.

She would be breaking that chain.

The thought affected her, and she felt the beginnings of regret and dangerous second thoughts.

"So what would you like to see next?" Vic asked as Lauren dragged herself back from her precarious thoughts.

"What do you recommend?" Alex addressed his question to her, seeming to ignore Vic.

"We can drive farther down the road to show you some of the other places and a few outbuildings," Lauren suggested.

"I thought we could go farther up into the hills on horseback. Get a feel for what that would be like. I was hoping you could come along," Alex said.

He slanted her an arch smile and added a touch on her arm that telegraphed his meaning.

He was flirting with her.

She was taken aback but recovered. She had to keep things professional.

Besides, his attention wasn't welcome or appreciated. She looked past him to Vic, who stood with his thumbs hooked through his belt loops in a classic cowboy pose.

Only she knew it wasn't fake. His hat was pulled low, shadowing his features. She couldn't read his expression, but she guessed he wasn't impressed with Alex.

"What do you think, Vic? Do you have time to saddle up some horses and go into the backcountry?" she asked.

"Sure. As long as Alex is up to an hour-long ride."

"I'll be okay," Alex said, still looking at Lauren, his smile deepening. "Especially if you come along."

Lauren tried not to roll her eyes. Instead she gave Alex a tight nod, then pushed herself away from the fence post. "Let's go, then."

Half an hour later, as she and Vic were saddling the horses, Alex wandered around the yard, looking at the house, the barns. But it seemed half his attention was on her.

As she slipped the cinch strap through the

ring, she caught Vic looking at her over top of Roany's saddle. "So what's your take on the guy?" Vic asked.

"What do you mean?"

"I think he's not interested in the Circle M as a ranch."

She tugged on the strap and threaded it through a last time, pulling as she did, striving to find the right words to express her own uncertainties and yet not give Vic false hope. "I know. I think he sees it as an investment, though I don't think he realized how large it was."

"You told him how many acres it was."

"When lots the size of your mother's garden are considered huge, you can't imagine how much land a ranch can encompass." She sighed, glancing back at Alex, who now stood, hands on his hips, smiling up at the house as if it met with his approval.

She had talked to Amy yesterday to reassure her that she would, indeed, send her share of the investment to her in a couple of months, once the will was satisfied and Alex had transferred the money.

Which he had assured her was not a problem.

"And you must do what you must do," he said, his voice quiet.

Lauren wasn't sure if he was mocking her or simply acknowledging her circumstances. Trouble was, she didn't like to think that he would want to hurt her.

She lowered the stirrup and rocked the saddle horn to make sure everything was secure, then ducked under the horse's lead rope to get the bridle.

"I'm sorry," Vic said as she passed him. Then, to her surprise, he caught her by the hand and turned her to look at him. "I shouldn't put pressure on you. It's just— I'm thinking that you're starting to like it here."

She suddenly found it difficult to breathe.

"I am. It's peaceful here," she said finally, fully aware of the callused warmth of his hand and how reluctant she was to remove hers. This was getting to be dangerous, she reminded herself even as she kept her hand where it was. The subtle connections between them were luring her into a place she had promised herself she would never go again.

"It can be," he said, his thumb making slow circles over her hand, making her heart speed up. "Winter can be harsh and wild, though. When the wind whips up snow and piles it into snowbanks, blocking off roads."

"I've never been here in the winter, except

when I was a little girl," she said, her breathless voice struggling to find equilibrium.

"It has its own beauty, though," Vic continued. "Its own moments when the sun comes out and the world looks like an endless blanket of white."

His voice and the pictures he sketched with it were beguiling, and Lauren imagined herself tucked away in her father's ranch house, looking out over blinding fields of white, a fire blazing in the hearth, a book on her lap.

It's a dream, her practical self told her. A foolish dream. How would she survive? How would she make a living?

She tugged her hand free and pulled herself away from Vic. She hurried to the tack shed, and in the quiet and gloom she caught her breath and regained her perspective.

She was growing dangerously attracted to Vic.

She couldn't allow this. Letting another man into her life was dangerous. Her father. Harvey. She had known them longer than she had known Vic and they both had proved to be untrustworthy. No way could she allow herself to be vulnerable again.

But unbidden came the questions Vic had asked her when they were coming back from the greenhouse. Questions no one had ever asked her—why she did what she did. Why she was an accountant.

She was good at it. It was her job. Her dream to start her own business.

But even as she repeated the words in her head, standing in this tack shed, the scents of old leather and saddle soap and the musky smell of horse blankets stirred other memories of rides into the hills. The freedom she felt here.

The peace.

She shook off the thoughts, grabbed Roany's halter and took a steadying breath. It was losing her father, she thought, that was making her feel so nostalgic. So vulnerable. She couldn't let herself get all emotional.

And with that pep talk fresh in her mind, she stepped out of the shed and ran straight into Alex.

"Whoa, there," he said, grabbing her arms to steady her. "There's no rush."

She gave him a tepid smile, pulling back. "Sorry. I don't want to keep Roany waiting," she said, holding up the bridle.

"I guess we don't want antsy horses on our ride." Then, thankfully, he lowered his hands.

She walked over to Roany and felt a moment's hesitation. It had been many years since she had bridled a horse, but she knew

Vic and Alex were watching and she wanted to prove herself competent.

Take your time, analyze the situation, then move with confidence.

Her father's advice returned to her. She took the headstall in one hand, the bit in the other, and with the hand holding the bit, inserted her finger and thumb on each side of Roany's mouth. She put pressure on his mouth, then he obligingly opened it and she neatly slipped the bit inside.

A few seconds later the bridle was on and buckled and Lauren felt in control of her world.

She led Roany to Alex, showed him how to get on, then returned to where Vic was buckling up Spot's bridle.

"Is she ready?"

Vic nodded, avoiding her eyes, and she wondered if he regretted that moment he had touched her.

As she mounted and followed Vic and Alex, she couldn't help but think how Alex's touch had done nothing for her.

But Vic's had left her breathless.

"From here you can see across the valley." Vic pointed out the Saddlebank River meandering through fields and groves of trees.

"Just to our right, about two miles down, is where Refuge Ranch starts, and beyond that the Fortier spread."

The land spread out below them and Lauren rested her hands on the horn of the saddle, letting her eyes sweep over the vista with its varying shades of green. The shadows of clouds moved over the undulating land. She heard the trill of a song sparrow, the eerie cry of a hawk circling overhead. And blended through it all the occasional lowing of cows.

An unexpected tranquility came over her and a peculiar happiness followed.

"I always loved coming up here," Lauren said to Vic, drawing in a cleansing breath and releasing it slowly.

"It's a beautiful view."

She glanced over at Alex, but he was frowning at his phone, reading something on the screen.

"The land goes right down to the river, doesn't it?" she asked, turning back to Vic.

"Some of the richest pastureland is right along the Saddlebank River. And it can carry a lot more cows than it does, but your dad would've needed more help to run them all. It's a great ranch, lots of potential."

Lauren was surprised at the admiration in Vic's voice. The way he leaned forward in the saddle, as if getting a better look at what lay below, showed a connection to the land that she envied. He was rooted here. He belonged here.

"What would you do with the ranch that my father didn't?" As soon as she asked the question, regret flashed through her. As if she was encouraging him to verbalize dreams that would never take place now.

But Vic smiled and pointed to the land below. "I'd break that pasture along the river and turn it into cropland."

"Wouldn't that leave you short on pasture?"

"The ranch isn't running to capacity. I've been holding back heifers to increase our herd over time. And when I get to the herd size I want, I would break the existing pastures into smaller ones and utilize rotational grazing to get more out of them." He glanced over at her and then gave her a laconic look. "But I guess that's all just a dream now, isn't it?"

Lauren didn't look away as regret and second thoughts scrabbled at her. She wanted to apologize, but that seemed moot. "Do you have the same view from your place?"

"No. Our ranch is on the other side of the road."

"It's beautiful, isn't it, Alex?" Lauren

avoided Vic's eyes, glancing over at Alex, but he was still busy with his phone.

She felt a moment's irritation and he must have sensed it, because he suddenly glanced over at her and slanted her a sheepish grin. "Just checking with my partner. He's shifting some stocks for me."

Lauren only nodded, recognizing his need to keep his finger on the pulse of his business.

Something she'd been neglecting the past two days. This morning she'd checked her phone and seen four text messages from Amy. She'd quickly answered them but left her phone in the house when she went out to help Vic.

She didn't want to be distracted on this ride, and she didn't want business to intrude.

"So, tell me some more about the ranch," Alex asked, dropping his phone back into his shirt pocket.

"This ranch can carry about eight hundred cow-calf pairs," Vic was saying, "and it currently has about four hundred acres in hay, which I was thinking—"

"What about the horses we saw on the yard? Would they come with the ranch?" Alex asked, interrupting Vic, turning to Lauren.

"I don't think so," Lauren said, shifting gears with Alex's change in topic. "Jodie and

Finn have been working with the horses, and I believe Finn wants to move them to his place when the ranch sells."

Jodie had been adamant that the horses not be sold with the ranch, and Lauren could understand her objections. They had good bloodlines. Her father had invested more money in the horses than in cattle, and Jodie and Finn were hoping to breed some more horses and train them.

"Too bad. Maybe I should talk to him. See if he'll sell me some. Be a good idea to have some horses available for when me and my friends come and stay here." He turned back to Vic. "How hard would it be to get some cabins built? Who could I talk to about that?"

"Jan Peter is a contractor based out of Saddlebank. He does good work," Vic said. "My brother works for him."

"Where would be a good place to build them? I don't know if I want to have guest cabins right on the main property."

"There is another yard site farther down the road," Vic said. "It used to be a separate ranch before Keith's father bought it out. There's an older house there. It has power and a well. That place could work."

As Vic spoke, Lauren had to dig back into

her memory, vaguely recalling visiting another yard site to do some cleanup around a house. She and her sisters had wanted to go exploring inside, but their father wouldn't let them. They'd had work to do and there had been no time for fun.

When they were a little older, she and Erin had saddled up the horses and gone riding down there. But the door of the house was locked, and the curtains were drawn over the window, and they were too afraid to break in. Erin had always said that someday she was going to live in that house, tucked in her own corner of the world.

Guess that isn't happening now, she thought, the weight of other people's expectations hanging on her shoulders. But Erin had remained uninvolved. It was up to her and Jodie to make the decisions. If Erin didn't want Lauren to sell, she hadn't made that known to her.

"I'd like to have a look at that place, too," Alex said as he took out his phone again. But this time he held it up and took a picture. He fiddled with his phone some more and looked up at Vic and Lauren. Smiling.

"This place would be a great investment." He nodded with a satisfied grin. "Now, let's go see that other yard."

* * *

Alex drove away, his shiny truck roaring off the yard, and honked the horn once as if saying one last goodbye.

Vic pushed his hat back on his head, trying hard not to begrudge the guy his fancy truck, his easy talk of getting financing to close the deal. As if it was simply a matter of shuffling money from one account to another.

But what bothered him most was his attitude toward the ranch. As if it was simply an investment. Some place to park his money until it increased.

He hadn't made a firm commitment to buying the place, and Vic knew he was dreaming, but part of him hoped Alex would change his mind.

He glanced at Lauren, who stood beside him, one arm folded over her stomach. Her other hand twisted a strand of her blond hair around and around her finger as she watched the dust cloud Alex's truck left behind waft over the yard.

"You seem disappointed," Vic said.

"Disappointed? No. Not really. I think he got a good idea of what he's getting into."

"He didn't give you an offer, though."

"Not yet, but I'm sure he'll take it. He told

me that it's the most promising property he's seen yet."

"He's looking at other places?" The thought ignited a tiny spark of hope.

"Just one other smaller ranch closer to Missoula. But he likes how this place is closer to the mountains. Likes how the land around here has increased in value."

Lauren and Alex had spent some time talking by his truck as Vic unsaddled the horses and brushed them down. He wasn't privy to that conversation, but he was surprised at the jealousy he felt when he saw Alex hug Lauren, hold her by the shoulders and give her another one of his flirtatious smiles.

Then he kissed her on the cheek and the jealousy began smoldering.

Stupid, he knew. She was never going to be part of his future in any way. But there it was.

He glanced at his watch. He had a couple of hours yet.

"I was wondering if I could have one last look through Keith's papers," Vic said, looking over at Lauren again.

"Of course," she said. "There's a few folders I haven't gone through, and yesterday we finally cracked the password on his computer."

"Really? What was it?"

"Our names." Lauren gave him a wistful smile. "Kind of touching."

"He did talk of you girls often."

"He wrote us each a letter before he died," Lauren told him.

"A final goodbye?" Vic asked.

"In a way. Apologies, as well. From a man who wasn't the easiest father, it's been an adjustment to read his regrets laid out in black and white. This from a man whose mantra was never apologize, never show weakness." She laughed. The sun caught glints of light in her hair. "My aunt gave us a bit of his background, however. And it helped us see him in a different light."

Her words seemed to fade. "Anyway, let's go through the rest of the papers first, then the computer. Hopefully…" Again her words drifted off and he wondered what she meant by *hopefully*.

Hopefully they would find something that would help him?

Or hopefully they wouldn't?

He pushed both thoughts aside as he followed her into the house. They went directly to the office and started sorting through the last of the files she had pulled out.

Twenty minutes later all the files had been gone through. Nothing.

"So, I guess we'll try the computer next," Lauren said, pulling up a chair to the desk, sensing Vic's disappointment. "Like I said, Jodie and I checked it out but couldn't find anything. You might have a better idea of what you're looking for."

Vic pulled the chair he'd been using beside hers. As he sat down, a stock picture of mountains came on the screen.

"Dad wasn't the most organized with the computer, and it's kind of old and has never been updated. But Jodie and I tried doing a search of lease agreements..." While she spoke, her fingers flew over the keyboard, and when she hit Return, a small beach ball–looking icon showed up and spun away.

Finally another window showed up with a list of files.

"You can see that some of these are emails and some of them are PDFs and a few documents. We looked through all of them but couldn't find anything resembling an agreement. Some of them are searches he's done on the internet that he might have bookmarked, so it looks like he was putting something together."

Vic leaned forward, as if getting six inches closer would give him more insight into what he was looking at.

"Would you have any idea of any other search terms we could use?"

"'Rent to own'?" Vic asked, scratching his forehead with his finger, trying to drag up any references Keith might have made that could help.

Once again Lauren's fingers flew over the keyboard.

"You clearly know how to handle a computer," Vic said, unable to keep the admiration out of his voice.

"What?" Lauren shot him a curious glance. "I'm just typing."

"Well, my typing is of the biblical sort," Vic said.

Lauren gave him a confused look.

"Seek and ye shall find," he said.

She laughed and the sound echoed in the office. It transformed her features. She held his gaze a beat longer than necessary and once again Vic felt the attraction he sensed was growing between them rise up.

"Did you enjoy yourself this afternoon?" he asked, hoping he didn't sound as breathless as he felt.

"I did. I've been out a few times by myself, but I never dared go that far. Not on my own and not on such a long ride." She smiled. "It was wonderful to see the valley looking so lush and green. To see all that space. I forgot how big the ranch was."

"It's a good size." He wanted to make a comment about Alex having lots to work with but didn't want to bring him into the moment.

"I never asked my father much about the history of the ranch. But was it this large when he inherited it from my grandfather?"

"Yes. It was. Your dad didn't expand it. He seemed content to let it be."

"Aunt Laura said he wasn't a rancher at heart."

"It wasn't what he wanted to do, but maybe he felt the pressure…maybe he thought it was what he was supposed to do."

She stopped, looking suddenly troubled.

And Vic's mind shifted back to the conversation they'd had when they were in the truck on the way back from the greenhouse. How she talked of her work as an accountant as something she'd fallen into. Something she had to do. When he'd asked her about her passion, it wasn't accounting that she spoke of.

This afternoon, working with the horses, riding the trail, looking out over the valley, he'd seen a peace come over her features that he'd only caught glimpses of before.

And he couldn't fight the feeling that whether she wanted to admit it or not, she belonged here more than she belonged any-where else.

He took a chance.

"Is that what this accounting business will be for you?"

Leaning back in her office chair, she shot him a puzzled glance. "What do you mean?"

"Do you see it the same way your father saw the ranch? Something you feel you should do, not something you have a passion for?"

She sucked in a quick breath, her eyes growing wide, a blaze of anger flashing in her eyes, and he thought he had gone too far.

But then she seemed to sag back against the chair, her hands clutching each other, her eyes looking away.

"It's an opportunity…it's a good business deal…" But her faltering words didn't hold the same assurance as the first time she had spoken them.

It sounded like she was working hard to convince herself of the rightness of her choices.

Then she shot him a wary glance. "Please don't tell me you're trying to make me doubt my decision because it will help you."

Vic knew how it must look to her. His sowing of doubt in her mind could work to his advantage.

He shook his head and took another chance, reaching out to touch her cheek. "I'm wondering if you're making a decision with your head or your heart. And I'm trying to put my opinions aside."

"Well, you'd be the first man in my life to do that." The bitter tone in her voice caught him by surprise.

"What do you mean?"

She waved off his question. "Nothing. Doesn't matter."

"Were you talking about your father?" He knew he was prying, but he wanted to know more about her. To deepen the connection he sensed building between them.

He leaned closer to Lauren, his arm resting along the back of her chair.

"Him and, well…a guy I was engaged to."

The canceled wedding.

"His name was—is—Harvey," Lauren continued. She didn't look away, but he saw the tightening of her jaw. Clearly it still bothered her.

"So what happened?" He kept his voice low and nonthreatening, his fingers lightly brushing her shoulder in commiseration.

Lauren looked away, concentrating on her hands wound tightly around each other. "Plans changed."

Her vague comment only increased his curiosity. "In what way?"

She lifted her chin, her eyes now hard, and Vic worried he might have gone too far. Pushed too hard.

"He got a chance to move to London and he suddenly decided that he didn't want me to come with him. So a week before our wedding, he called it off. Jodie was with me when it happened." She shot him a frown. "She didn't tell you?"

"Guess it wasn't mine to know." Vic let his hand rest on her shoulder and gave it a light squeeze.

She sighed, her fingers unwinding from each other. "It happened two years ago. We'd been engaged for four. I kept waiting for him to commit. Kept pushing him to make a decision. He finally decided on a date, then he got this job opportunity." She paused, then shook her head. "I wasn't a part of the decision. He decided that he wanted to go on his own. Dropped me and—" She stopped there. "However, he only managed to reinforce a lesson that I learned the hard way from my father and my last boss."

"And that was?"

She tilted her head to one side, as if examining him, deciding what she should or shouldn't tell him.

"That I have to take care of myself. That no one else is going to do that for me."

Vic heard the steely conviction in her voice. He sensed there was more to the story, but he also sensed he wasn't going to get anything else from her.

At least not now.

But it gave him an insight into her need to sell the ranch.

"Well, you need to know that not all men are the same," he said, his hand still cupping her shoulder.

She looked at him. Really looked at him, her features softening as their eyes met. "I'd like to believe that. I really would." Her words were quiet, and as their eyes held, Vic felt the attraction growing between them.

Then he gave in to an impulse, leaned closer and gently brushed his lips over hers.

She didn't move. Just sat perfectly still. Had he misread the situation? But to his surprise and joy, she slipped her hand around his neck and returned his kiss, her fingers tangling in his hair, her mouth warm and responsive.

Slowly they separated and he laid his forehead against hers. Her breath was warm on his face.

He knew he had shifted much with this kiss.

Trouble was, he wasn't sure where it would end.

Chapter Eight

Lauren knew she should pull back. At least her logical self knew she should. But the part of her that yearned for Vic's presence kept her close to him, one hand on his neck, her other on his broad, warm shoulder.

Now what?

The question swirled through her mind and she wasn't sure what to do with it. Alex had just left with a promise to call her. Her plans hadn't changed and yet…

She drew away, her hands drifting down over his chest, her fingers trailing over his shirt, and then, reluctantly, she pulled back.

She didn't want to feel confused. Didn't want to feel vulnerable. Things were moving too quickly. Too much was happening at once. And yet all she wanted was for him to kiss her again.

She turned away, swallowing down her misgivings, focusing on the computer screen. "So let's try…" She cleared her throat and tried again. "Let's try that other search term you were talking about."

She typed in "rent to own" and again the spinning beach ball came up, followed by a list of files.

Lauren scrolled through these as well, slowly shaking her head. "Sorry. No documents, no PDFs, just a few internet searches he bookmarked. But I can't find anything."

"And you're sure we've gone through all the papers?"

"I'm sure." Lauren leaned forward a moment, then shook her head, looking again. "Sorry. Nothing."

Lauren typed in a few more search terms, giving it a few more tries, but she couldn't find anything. She wished she could. Wished that something would turn up.

After her ride with Vic and listening to him talking about the ranch, her doubts about her plans had been intensified. She wasn't so sure she wanted Alex owning this ranch. Turning it from a working ranch into a vacation spot for him and his friends for only a few weeks of the year. Looking at it as strictly an investment that he could get rid of to another rich friend if the time was right. Though her father hadn't wanted to be a rancher, she'd heard about the legacy of the Circle M. And seeing the place through Vic's eyes gave her another perspective.

She turned her chair to face him, giving him a careful smile.

"I'm sorry, but I can't find anything."

He shoved his hand through his hair in what she assumed was a gesture of frustration.

"So, what now?" he asked, his voice taking on a hard edge.

"I'm not sure," she said, surprising herself with her vague answer. When she first came to the ranch she'd been so sure of what she wanted.

But now?

"But I do want to thank you for taking me and Alex around on the ranch. I enjoyed it."

A vague smile teased his lips. "I'm glad. I don't know how much Alex enjoyed it, though. He seemed more interested in his phone than in what we were showing him."

"When you're running a business, you need to stay in touch." Which was a reminder to herself to get in touch with Amy. Find out how things were going with the business.

But not now, she thought, feeling a wistful sweetness at being with Vic. For the first time in a long time, she felt as if the cycles of frenetic activity in her life had been put aside. She felt she could slip through the day, enjoying the moments as they came instead of always looking ahead to the next one and worrying how it would turn out, tweaking, adjusting and shifting so it could.

"At any rate, I was thankful for the tour. It was fun to go out riding."

"You seemed comfortable around the horses," he said. "Maybe we should go out again sometime."

She grinned at the thought. "I think I would enjoy that."

Then he reached to brush her hair away from her face, tucking it behind her ear.

It was a casual gesture but spoke to a growing intimacy between them that she wasn't sure what to do with.

But for now, she didn't want it to end. His eyes seemed to smolder and she sat perfectly still, expectation humming between them.

His head moved a fraction, and before she could stop herself, she moved to meet him.

Then the porch door crashed open and a voice called out, "Hello? Anybody home?"

Jodie.

Lauren stifled a sigh of annoyance, then gave Vic a regretful smile.

"Guess my sister is back."

"Lousy timing," he said, his finger trailing down her cheek.

Then he pushed himself to his feet and grabbed his cowboy hat from the filing cabinet. "So, I guess we'll see each other around?"

"I sure hope so," Lauren said, standing up, folding her arms over her stomach.

"You coming to the rodeo on Friday?"

"Absolutely," she returned.

"I'll see you then." And the smile he gave her was like a promise.

"So did you and Vic find anything connected to that lease agreement he's been looking for?" Jodie asked later, after Vic had gone and Lauren had helped her cart in all the groceries and wedding stuff.

Lauren dropped the last of the bags on the kitchen counter and began putting the groceries away in the cupboard and refrigerator. "No. Unfortunately."

"Unfortunately. That's an interesting choice of words."

Trust her sister to pounce on a single comment and braid an entire conversation out of it.

"Unfortunately for Vic," Lauren amended. "I think the computer was his last hope at finding something to substantiate his claim."

Jodie sighed as she set a handful of shopping bags on the kitchen table. "And did your guy Alex Rossiter come today?"

"Not my guy. Just the potential buyer."

It wasn't too hard to see by the grim set of Jodie's mouth what she thought of it, but as quickly as her grimace came, it left. Lauren felt again the weight of expectation and behind that, doubt over her decision. She knew Jodie supported her, but she also knew that the longer Jodie stayed here, the less inclined she was to sell the ranch.

Trouble was, Lauren felt the same. And the memory of Vic's kiss didn't help her resolve any.

"Did Vic get the haying done?" Jodie asked, moving on to safer topics.

"Yes. He did. He said he had to haul the bales back to his ranch, but that would probably happen next week."

"The garden is looking good," Jodie said as she unpacked the bags she had set on the table. "I love how they brighten up the place. You have a real knack for that. Makes the place look more like a home. I should get you to do some landscaping on Finn's place—my future home," she said. Her voice took on a dreamy tone that used to make Lauren feel a mixture of happiness for her sister blended with a touch of envy.

But now?

She reached up to touch her lips, as if to see if she could still feel Vic's lips on hers.

"I think that could be fun" was all she said. "Now show me what you decided on."

Jodie gave her a searching look, then a slow smile crawled over her lips. "You seem happier today. Was it because you spent the day with Vic?"

Lauren's heart jumped in her chest. She wasn't sure she was ready to bring all this out into the open. Not sure she wanted to discuss with her sister the confusion that gripped her.

She knew exactly what Jodie would say and on which side she would come down on. Lauren knew she needed to make her decision on her own without any outside influence.

"I'm just glad that our tour with Alex went well" was all she said.

Jodie's smile faded and she nodded. "Of course."

Lauren felt like a fraud, but she couldn't talk about Vic. Not yet. Not when she didn't know herself what she wanted.

"So tell me what you found for the table decorations."

With a bright smile Jodie grabbed the first bag and pulled out a box of flameless candles. And then some fabric for table runners and a host of other items.

The wedding was being held at Finn's place. It was to be a small affair in December with a Christmas theme, but Jodie still wanted it to be classy, she'd said.

"We still need to decide what you and Erin are wearing," Jodie said. "And I wanted you to come with me to Aunt Laura's to make a final decision on the flowers. I also need to make a payment on that wedding dress we found."

"Too bad I didn't keep my dress. You could have worn it," Lauren said with a wry tone.

Jodie bit her lip and rested her hand on Lauren's shoulder. "I'm sorry. I keep forgetting that this is hard for you."

Lauren just shook her head. "I'm happy for you. Truly. And every day I'm away from Harvey I realize how wrong he was for me."

Mostly because she now had another standard by which to judge him. A man who, even though it put her in conflict with him, put the needs of his family first.

A man of integrity who was willing to help.

Who kissed her.

A flush warmed her cheeks and she looked away, frustrated that such a simple thing could create this reaction. She'd been kissed before. Nothing new.

But not by a man like Vic.

"Harvey was wrong for you, and though I'm so sad that he called off the wedding, better that than a divorce like Mom and Dad had to deal with."

Lauren turned a roll of ribbon over in her hands, trying to formulate her wayward thoughts.

"Do you worry if you're able to do this? Get married?"

Jodie grinned, but when she caught Lauren's eyes, she grew serious. "What do you mean?"

Lauren turned the ribbon over again, picking at the price tag with her index finger. "Mom couldn't manage. I couldn't. Your old boyfriend Lane dumped you. Erin claims she never wants to be married…"

She let the last of the sentence fade away as she thought of the most recent text she had received from her twin sister a couple of days ago. Talking about faithless men and how marriage was a farce.

Oh, Erin, what is going on in your life? Why won't you tell us?

Jodie took the roll of ribbon away from Lauren and took her hands in her own. "Of course I'm concerned. Getting married is a big commitment. I haven't had the best experiences with guys, either. But I believe in Finn and I especially believe that God has blessed our relationship. That's what holds us together. And the fact that I know that together we can go to God in prayer with the things that concern us. That we can hold hands and put everything in God's care."

Jodie squeezed Lauren's hands. "From what I hear about Mom and Dad, that didn't happen, and I know that Harvey didn't go to church. And Lane, well, he attended church, but I can't think of any time we prayed together. But Finn and I do. I think that's what makes the difference, and that is what helps me believe this will work."

Lauren held her sister's earnest gaze, sensing her conviction and recognizing the truth in what she was saying. "I know that you love him and that he is a good person..." She stopped herself, knowing that she had to be careful.

"There's a *but* hovering there, waiting to

come out, except in your case it would be a *however*," Jodie said with a quick laugh.

Lauren gave her an apologetic smile. "Doesn't matter."

"Spill it," Jodie urged.

Still Lauren hesitated, knowing she would be showcasing her own insecurities if she continued.

"Please. You never said much after Harvey canceled the wedding and took off for London. I remember helping you cancel events, return stuff, sell your dress. I know it was hard for you, but you never complained at all."

"What good would it have done?" Lauren asked, putting the red ribbon she'd been toying with back in the bag. "It was over. I made a monumental mistake."

"What mistake? Dating Harvey?"

"Trusting Harvey." She shrugged. "I don't know if I dare let myself do that with any man again."

Jodie gave her a sympathetic look. "I can understand that. But trust is a major part of any relationship. And I can guard my heart and keep it to myself, or take a chance and trust Finn. And I have chosen to trust him. Because I know I can. Because I know Finn will do anything for me. Make a sacrifice for me."

Lauren was envious of her sureness, but as she listened to her sister, a cold reality unfurled.

"What?" Jodie prompted. "You look like you've had a major breakthrough.

"I just realized that none of the men who had been important in my life have ever done that," Lauren said. "None of them have ever made any kind of sacrifice for me. Not Dad. Not Harvey. Interesting."

"Interesting and kind of sad, isn't it?" Jodie said. "I could say the same thing until I met Finn."

Then Jodie got up and gave her a quick hug, pulling back and holding her shoulders. "When the right man comes along, I believe you'll know you can trust him."

"Maybe," Lauren said in a noncommittal tone. And unbidden came a memory of Vic driving her to town, helping her with her car.

She shook off the memory, knowing how dangerous it was. She had to stay focused on her plans.

"So where do you want to store this stuff?" she asked, gathering up the spools of ribbon and putting them back in the bag.

But that night she lay in her bedroom, staring up at the ceiling, thinking about what Jodie had said. Thinking about trust, reliving the day. Smiling as she thought of their ride up into the mountains, feeling her heart shift in her chest as she kept returning to that moment in the office when Vic kissed her and her world tilted.

You can't let yourself be vulnerable again, she told herself. *You can't let anyone else determine the direction of your life. You're in charge. Have to be.*

But somehow those words taunted her with their empty certainty. She thought of the sermon she'd heard on Sunday. How the pastor had spoken of how we want to control our lives and what a foolish notion that is. How little control we actually have.

And, at the same time, how important it was to place every plan we make in God's perspective and see it through the eyes of eternity. What will last, what will persevere?

And what will glorify God?

Lauren tossed over onto her side again. Was she being selfish? Was she focusing too much on the things of this earth and not seeking God first?

She turned onto her back, staring up the ceiling of the room that had belonged to her over two months of the year for nine years.

She remembered the many dreams she had spun here. Dreams of being on her own, away from family and obligations, and trying to keep everyone happy.

Was it so wrong to want to take care of herself? Trusting other people to do so had been a huge mistake. She knew Jodie wanted her to keep the ranch, but Jodie didn't need it. Erin didn't seem to care. So it was up to her.

And Vic wanted it for his brother. Needed it for his brother.

But surely that couldn't be reason enough for her to give up on her own dreams and plans. Dean had Vic to take care of him. Whom did she have?

She closed her eyes and breathed out a prayer, the only thing she knew she could do right now.

Guide my decisions, Lord, she prayed. *Help me to make decisions that will glorify You.*

But even as she prayed, part of her held on to her own ideas. Trouble was, she wasn't entirely sure she trusted God, either.

Chapter Nine

Vic tightened the cinch on his horse, checked the rigging, rope and bridle. Once he was sure everything was secure, he adjusted the padded leather chaps he wore to protect his legs. Behind him he heard the clang of horses' hooves against the metal fences outside, the bawling of steers, waiting to be ridden.

The day was rodeo perfect. Plenty of sunshine and enough of a breeze to keep the bugs off the animals.

Ahead of him, he heard the crowd gathering in the stands, the country music echoing in the arena.

Ten minutes before showtime.

Then a sudden attack of nerves was unwelcome and surprising, as memories slammed into his mind.

Dean falling off the horse. The cry of agony as his leg got caught in the fence.

That one moment that changed everything.

Could he really do this?

Every time he rode out into the arena, he felt the responsibility of the care of the cowboys and the stock. But Lauren would be in the crowd this evening.

Distraction or welcome presence?

He paused before getting on, taking in the building's energy, the contestants gathering, the whinny of horses, the bellowing of steers and bulls.

The energy and the possibility that things could go well or go very wrong.

Help me be strong, Lord, he prayed, resting his head on his saddle before he mounted. *Help me stay focused. Help me to keep my concentration on what I need to do.*

Because knowing Lauren was in the crowd made a difference whether he wanted to admit it or not.

He drew in a deep, calming breath, the smells of dirt, horses and hot dogs bringing up older and better memories. Those were the ones he had to cling to, he reminded himself. The cowboys he rescued. The horses and bulls he got safely into the back pens. His unsung successes that were part of every rodeo pickup man's story.

"Vic Moore. Glad to see you here," a high-pitched voice called out.

Vic turned around to face a young man in his late twenties. Tall, lanky, his upper lip curved over a chew of tobacco, his black cowboy hat square on his head, wearing a plaid shirt and Wrangler blue jeans—Walden Proudfoot was the embodiment of a rodeo cowboy and one of the best pickup men in the business.

Walden slapped Vic on the shoulder, nodding his approval of his presence. "So glad you're working with me. I missed you."

"I missed being here."

"When I found out you were partnering with me, I knew I was in good hands."

Vic laughed, thankful for the confidence Walden had in him.

"How's Dean doing?"

"Still a struggle."

"He miss rodeoing?"

Vic shook his head. "He's never mentioned it." The focus of Dean's anger and bitterness seemed to be his disability more than his inability to ride broncs again.

"That's too bad. He was a solid rider."

"And what about you? When are you going

to quit this game?" Vic asked, steering the conversation to a safer topic.

"I don't know. Hauling five horses around from rodeo to rodeo gets tiring and expensive. I'm done by the end of the season, but each time spring rolls around, I get the itch."

"It's in your blood or not," Vic admitted. "How's your brother Ziggy doing? Has he ever finished in the money?"

"Nope. Still a donator."

Vic had to laugh at the term given to cowboys who never made any money but kept competing. He asked after a few more friends who had ridden the circuit with them, swapped a few more stories about other rodeos.

And then a voice booming over the mic called out the individual competitors of the events. They each came out to stand in a circle facing the audience.

Vic rode out with Walden when their names were announced, cantering their horses around the arena, hats lifted in greeting.

He scanned the crowd, heard his name and saw a woman with dark hair, standing, waving both arms, cupping her hand around her mouth and whistling. Jodie.

What a character.

But it was the reserved blonde beside her

who snagged his attention. He inclined his head toward her and then, a second later, she was out of his sight.

Then the singing of the national anthem was announced. Two members of the drill team came out, cantering around the ring, the Stars and Stripes and the flag of the association following.

After the anthem was sung, the cowboys all ran out, and with a roar and a blare of music, the rodeo was underway.

Vic took up his position to the right of the bareback chutes, pulled his hat down, recoiled his rope and quieted his horse.

Then with a clang of the gate, the first horse and rider burst out of the chute.

The next hour was a combination of waiting, anticipation humming through him and his horse, and an eruption of action, watching, reading, pacing the animals, and getting the rider on the back of his horse and setting him down if need be.

Vic settled easily back into the routine, surprised at how much he had missed the excitement. The expectation. The sudden quick moves as he paced the broncs.

He switched horses when the calf ropers and the steer wrestlers worked from the other end of the arena, hazing the steers. He helped chase a few of them back to the pens and between times managed to catch a few glimpses of Lauren. She was leaning forward, watching, intent.

Just like she did everything else, he thought, shifting on his horse as he returned to his position while the horses were brought into the bucking chutes.

He wondered if she thought about the kiss they'd shared as much as he had.

The announcer called out the next event.

Saddle bronc.

The one that had put his brother in the hospital.

He shoved his hat down on his head and, as he usually did before any cowboy was ready to go, uttered a quick but sincere prayer.

Lord, help me to do my job, stay focused, and keep the cowboy and horse safe.

Then the cowboys holding the chute gate got the nod from the cowboy on the horse. The gate swung open and with a lunge the horse exploded into the arena.

Vic pulled his horse back to give the bronc room, watching as the horse bucked, keeping his attention on the rider and the movements of the horse. The bronc sunfished, spun, and just before the buzzer went, Vic and Walden rode alongside the horse to release the bucking strap and get the rider off. But Vic could see the rider was in trouble. His foot had slipped too far into the stirrup.

Vic's heart jumped; adrenaline kicked in. He signaled to Walden to take care of the horse as he came up abreast of the rider, now dangling down from the saddle.

Vic moved his horse in as close as he could get, trusting his horse to do his job while Vic did his.

"Grab my hand," he called out to the cowboy. He reached down, almost coming off his own saddle as his horse paced the bucking horse, not fazed by its tossing head and frantic movements.

The cowboy tried, but the erratic actions of the horse made it impossible.

"I got ya, I got ya," Vic called out in encouragement.

Then he leaned down again just as the bronc took a sudden turn toward his own horse, and he and the dangling cowboy were crushed between the two racing animals.

"What's happening? What's going on?" Lauren stood, leaning closer, watching the frightening scene unfolding below. All she saw were horses racing alongside each other, cowboys scattering as the horses came toward them. Vic was leaning so far over she couldn't believe he could stay in his saddle.

"The rider got his foot hung up," Finn was saying, his voice tense. "He can't get out."

The other pickup man was hauling hard on the lead rope to pull the horse back. He leaned back and snapped the bucking strap off the animal, but still the horses ran around the arena in a clump of legs and bodies.

"Where's Vic? Where's Vic?" Lauren wanted to run down and leap over the walls to help, even though she knew she could do nothing.

Her heart thundered in her chest. Her hands grew clammy. What was going on? Why wasn't Vic coming up?

Then another cowboy on horseback came into the arena, followed by a group of other competitors.

"Stay with him. Vic, stay with him," she heard Finn muttering over the fearful cries from the audience around her.

She couldn't watch, but she couldn't look away. It all happened so fast and yet it seemed it would never end.

Finally the horses slowed down and as they did, Vic sat up, his hand clutching the bright

red shirt of the bronc rider, dragging him onto
the back of his horse. While the rider clung,
Vic reached down again and then, amazingly,
the cowboy's foot was free. The saddle bronc
gave a shake of his head as if to say this was
all in a day's work, then trotted off, led by
Walden, the other pickup man.

Lauren sat back on the bench, her heart
still banging like a drum in her chest. He had
come so close, she thought, remembering the
sight of the horse's dangerous hooves flailing
about, inches from Vic's head. It could have
ended so badly.

Thank You, Lord, she prayed, pulling another breath. *Thank You for saving Vic.*

Everyone in the crowd cheered as the competitor slipped off the back of Vic's horse and
raised his hat to the crowd.

Then limped off to the chute area.

Vic patted his horse and Lauren saw his
shoulders come up as if pulling in a deep
breath of relief. His head turned just enough,
his eyes scanning the crowd, and then he
seemed to see her. He gave her a quick nod
and then turned his horse back, ready for the
next competitor.

"That was too close," Lauren said, her
hands pressed to her chest, her heart racing.

"I thought Vic was going to fall off that horse. That was so scary."

"Vic's one of the best riders I know," Jodie assured her, putting her arm around her shoulders as if in support. "He knows what he's doing. See how he managed to get that guy off the horse? Bet he hardly broke a sweat."

Lauren nodded, knowing Jodie was right, but her terror surprised her. Watching Vic now, adjusting his rope and tugging on his gloves, settling himself in his saddle, he seemed the epitome of calm. A quiet center in the middle of the madness going on in the arena.

But her hands and knees were still weak, her legs still trembling.

Then she caught Finn's grin.

"That's rodeo," he said. "Ten minutes of prep followed by eight seconds of panic."

"The panic seemed longer than eight seconds," she said, her voice shaky.

"Vic was in charge the whole time," Finn assured her.

Lauren felt herself relax, but at the same time the depth of her reaction surprised her. Even dismayed her a bit. Vic meant more to her than she realized.

"He's good at what he does," Jodie said. "You don't need to worry."

"I wasn't…worried." But her heart wasn't slowing down, a solid testament to her concern.

"Well, you seemed worried." Jodie nudged her with her elbow. Then she got up. "But all this excitement made me hungry. I'm getting some fries. Anyone else want some? Lauren?"

"We just ate," Lauren said, giving her a frown.

"Soup and salad." Jodie wrinkled her nose and shot Finn a pained look. "Lauren made me eat carrot and chickpea soup and quinoa salad, if you can imagine. No bread. No dessert. I need a major infusion of starch and fat. You sure you don't want any?" she asked Finn.

Finn shook his head, as well. "I'm good. Had a delicious veggie burger at the Grill and Chill."

"You did not," Jodie said with an incredulous tone, giving him a poke.

"I did. Brooke told me she was going to get George to cook more healthy options and give people more choices on the menu."

"A veggie burger? My fiancé is eating a veggie burger? Can't believe George got convinced to do that."

"Brooke has some pull these days with him."

"Do you think she has enough to get him to pull an engagement ring out of his pocket?"

"Oh, goodness, not that soap opera again?" Finn asked, a pained note in his voice.

Lauren frowned at Finn as he rolled his eyes. "What soap opera?" she asked.

Jodie just smiled her indulgence at her fiancé, giving him a patronizing look. "He's talking about the ongoing relationship between Brooke and George Bamford. Owner of the Grill and Chill."

"Brooke Dillon?"

"Yes. Gordon and Brooke's romance has been years in the making. Everyone in Saddlebank has been watching it develop."

"I think I remember her. She's good friends with Keira Bannister, isn't she?"

"Yep. And I worked with her decorating for the concert last month."

Lauren couldn't help but feel some guilt at the mention of Jodie's concert. She should have come, but she'd been hanging on to her job by her fingernails, working late all the time to satisfy her boss, doing everything she could to keep her job.

Not that it had done her any good.

"Anyhow, it looks like things are on between them again," Jodie continued. "And I have to go get some fries before I faint from carb deprivation." Then she jogged down the stairs toward the concessions, her dark hair bouncing behind her.

Lauren smiled at her sister, then turned her attention back to the arena, thankful for the little interlude that helped settle her racing heart.

Vic was loping his horse around the arena, chasing the last bronc toward the chutes.

Then he turned his horse around, head up, as if he was looking for her.

Their eyes met and she felt a tingle. Then he turned and got ready for the next competitor.

A few more cowboys competed, and while they did, Finn explained some of the finer points of the event. How the cowboy had to be positioned when they came out of the chute. How they were marked for their spurring and how the horses were marked for their bucking.

"The combined points gives the cowboy his score," he said, just as another cowboy was bucked off.

Thankfully the following rides were less dramatic, though Lauren had to admit they were all thrilling. She cheered as hard as anyone when a cowboy made his eight seconds and called out her disappointment when one didn't.

But as interesting as the rides were, her eyes consistently shifted to where Vic was working. The flash and drama came from the cowboys with their decorated and fringed chaps, their dramatic rides and dismounts or dumps. But the entire time Vic and Walden rode along the edges of the area, swooping in on their solid and unfazed horses, coming alongside to help a cowboy off, chase horses away.

"I noticed Vic is riding a different horse this time," she said to Finn. "When he first started he was on a pinto horse."

"And he'll probably be riding a couple more before the events are all done," Finn said, leaning forward, his elbows resting on his knees, his program rolled up in his hands as he scanned the grounds. "Those horses get a good workout, and you need them fresh and alert. It's not uncommon for a pickup man to go through four or five horses over the course of the evening."

"They seem so calm," Lauren commented as she watched Vic and his horse, waiting at the end of the arena. "The horses."

"They have to be," Finn said. "But they also need a bit of kick to them."

Lauren was confused. "What do you mean?"

"They have to run alongside a snorty horse full of adrenaline and stay in charge. Not be afraid to push back if the saddle bronc or bareback bronc wants to challenge them. And they have to be able to do all that in a noisy arena with all kinds of other things going on and still respond to what the rider wants."

"Does Vic work as a pickup man often?" she asked, watching as he successfully roped a horse that wouldn't come back and led it around the arena toward the alley leading to the back pens. With a skillful flip of his wrist he got the rope off and was now coiling it up, his movements slow, unhurried.

"Only once in a while since Dean's accident," Finn said.

"Vic seems to blame himself for that," Lauren said.

"When a cowboy gets hurt, I think the pickup men always look back and wonder what they could have done differently. In Vic's case it was his own brother that got hurt. But from what I heard, I doubt Vic could have changed the outcome no matter what he did."

Then Finn nudged her with his elbow. "And why does this matter to you so much?"

Lauren knew the flush warming her neck and face was a giveaway, but she kept her eyes on Vic. "I hate to see someone take responsibility for something that they don't have to."

"Especially if his name is Vic?"

Lauren wasn't going to get pulled into that tangle. So she said nothing.

"I think he likes you," Finn added, rubbing his square jaw with his forefinger and giving her a knowing look. "And Vic's not the kind of guy to show his hand too quick. Not when it comes to women. Not since Tiffany."

Lauren pressed her hands between her knees, reminding herself that it shouldn't matter to her if he'd had a romantic past. She did, too, after all.

But she was also a weak woman, and the memory of Vic's kiss, the touch of his hand on her face, elicited emotions she hadn't felt in a long time.

"Who was Tiffany?" The question slipped out before she could stop herself.

"A girl that caused a lot of complication in Vic's life," Finn said. "She was dating Dean for a while. Then she dumped him, hoping to get together with Vic. She and Vic had dated a few years before that. She was in the arena the day that Dean had his accident. But she left right after that."

"Why?"

Finn shook his head, tapping the rolled-up program on his knee. "Vic wasn't interested in her after that. But between getting dumped and the accident, Dean became a bitter young man. And it kept Vic shy of women since then." Then Finn gave her a wry smile. "Until you."

Lauren swallowed down a surprising jealousy, but at the same time she felt a renewed flutter at Finn's insinuation. She wanted to brush it off and tell him he was crazy.

But just then Vic rode past. The event was over and he was walking his horse along the fence. And he was watching her.

She saw a faint smile on his lips, and her heart gave an answering beat. She had to catch herself from lifting up her hand in a wave.

"Next up, ladies' barrel racing," Jodie announced as she plonked herself down between Lauren and Finn. She carried a large cardboard tray loaded with French fries topped with a bright red mountain of ketchup. "And don't you dare touch my fries," she warned, glancing from Finn to Lauren.

"Trust me, the way you've bathed those in ketchup, I'm not tempted," Lauren said.

"So you got over your scare?" Jodie asked, popping a fry in her mouth.

"What scare?" Lauren pretended not to know what her sister was talking about.

"Oh, c'mon. When Vic dived down to get that rider, you turned as white as a marshmallow."

Lauren wasn't sure how to respond to her sister's teasing. On one hand it made her smile. She and her sisters used to tease each other mercilessly if there was any hint of attraction to any guy. Usually it became a chance to huddle up in someone's bedroom when Gramma was asleep. Or, when they were at the ranch, while their father worked the night shift.

They would giggle, analyze and rhapsodize, and either encourage if they approved or discourage if they didn't.

She knew Jodie approved of Vic. And that she hadn't cared for Harvey. Somehow that seemed to add another layer to her changing emotions for Vic.

"Oh, look, there's Aunt Laura finally come to join us."

"Where?" Lauren asked.

"Look for the fluorescent plaid shirt and pink shorts," Jodie said, standing up to wave.

And sure enough, there Aunt Laura was, making her way up the stairs, holding down her purple cowboy hat with one hand, a bag of popcorn in the other.

"Where does she find getups like that?" Finn asked as Aunt Laura slipped past the people at the end of the row. "I didn't know boot companies even made purple cowboy boots."

"Hey, Auntie," Lauren said, when their aunt joined them.

"Hello, my dear girls. And Finn," Aunt Laura said, giving Lauren a quick hug and Finn a salute with her bag of popcorn.

"How was your day?" Lauren asked.

"Not too bad. More lookie loos at the shop than buyers, unfortunately." Aunt Laura sighed, giving Lauren a nudge. "I should get you to make up some arrangements for me. I'm sure they'd fly out of the cooler. You have a knack."

Lauren waved off her compliments, then Jodie spoke up.

"The horse Finn trained is going to be competing next," Jodie said to her aunt. "You came just in time."

"Excellent. Is it competing on its own, this well-trained horse?"

Jodie gave her an arch look, catching the irony in her aunt's voice. "Yes. Sans rider.

Finn trained it so well it can run barrels on its own."

"This I have to see," Aunt Laura said, folding her hands on her lap, winking at Lauren.

Then a woman sat down behind Finn, and as she leaned forward, Lauren saw a flash of blond hair and caught the scent of almond perfume.

"Hey, Finn, do you think your nag stands a chance against the one I trained?" the woman teased.

Lauren glanced back and grinned when she saw who it was.

Her distant cousin Heather also trained barrel-racing horses. Lauren guessed that Finn and Heather had some healthy competition going on.

"Hey, Heather," Lauren said, lifting her hand in a wave of greeting. "It's been a while."

"No kidding," Heather said, patting her on the shoulder. "I heard you were back in town. So great to see you. We'll have to catch up sometime."

"That sounds like a plan," Lauren said. The sight of her cousin brought back many good memories of times spent at the Bannister ranch.

"I not only think my well-broke and intelligent horse will do better than the one you took under your wing, I know it," Finn said, a challenge in his voice.

"You two do realize that someone has to ride these trained animals," Aunt Laura chimed in. "And that a good rider can make a poor horse compete better and that no amount of training can make up for a poor rider."

"Aunt Laura, shush," Heather said, placing her finger on her lips. "You start spreading those kinds of rumors and you'll put me and Finn right out of a job."

They all chuckled, then turned their attention to the first competitor. In spite of the teasing, they all cheered each competitor on as the girls went racing down the arena, guiding their horses around the barrels, leaning so far in that Lauren thought they might fall off.

"Sounds like the horse you trained is up next," Jodie said to Finn, giving him a thumbs-up as the announcer called out the name of the next competitor. "Here's hoping it doesn't balk."

"Don't even say that word out loud," Finn warned.

Jodie pressed her finger to the wrinkle above the bridge of his nose, then fluttered her fingers. "Frown, be gone."

And when Finn laughed and gave Jodie a quick kiss, Lauren felt another tinge of envy.

That's what she wanted, she told herself. What Jodie and Finn had. That easy give-and-take. She looked back at Heather and John, who were sitting close together, then at her aunt sitting on the other side of her. She felt surrounded by people she knew. A community.

She wanted this, too.

And what about your business? Isn't that what you really want?

Panic swirled up in her at the questions. She couldn't be wrong about the business, could she? Because if she didn't have that, what did she have?

She looked away from Finn and Jodie, her hands clenched as she glanced around the arena.

Then she saw Vic. Perched on the top rail of the fence by the bucking chutes to watch the barrel racing. He wore his hat pushed back on his head, his gloves in his hands, his elbows resting on his knees as he leaned ahead.

He looked over to where she was sitting and straightened, a smile slipping over his features.

Lauren felt a shift in her perspective. The hum of possibilities.

Did she dare put it all in this man's hands?

Chapter Ten

Vic led the last of his horses into the trailer, ran its lead rope through the metal loop on the side and secured it with a bowline knot. He gave it a tug to make sure it was solid, then walked around the horse, running his hands over its rump to make it aware of his position. The other horses whinnied, sensing they were headed home.

Vic jumped out of the trailer and as he grabbed the door, he saw a welcome sight.

Lauren, followed by Finn and Jodie, was walking through the dusty temporary pens toward him. Her blue jeans were snug, her white shirt loose and her hair hung around her face in a blond cloud, softening her features.

As did her welcoming smile.

"Great job tonight, Vic," Finn said as they

joined him. "That catch was one in a million. It's probably all over the internet already."

Vic just grinned as he closed the squeaking back gate of the horse trailer and latched it shut. "I doubt that."

"You kidding?" Finn said, clapping his hand on Vic's shoulder. "I'm sure there were at least a dozen phones trained on you. You'll be a YouTube wonder."

Vic just laughed, looking past Finn to Lauren, who had hung back but was watching him.

Just like he was watching her.

"You bringing your horses back to your ranch tonight?" Jodie asked, tucking her arm through Finn's. "Aren't you working again tomorrow?"

"Just for slack. Devlin is coming in tomorrow night, so I'm off."

"Big plans for tomorrow night, then?"

Vic wished his eyes didn't slip toward Lauren, and when he caught Finn's smirk, he wished he had more self-control.

"Jodie and I should go," Finn was saying. "I need to go congratulate Adelaide on her win tonight."

Then they were gone, and Vic and Lauren were alone.

In the ensuing quiet, Vic felt suddenly self-conscious. Like some goofy teenager in the presence of his crush.

"That was quite something tonight," Lauren said. "The way you rescued that rider."

Vic shrugged off her praise, uncomfortable with his moment of fame. The young bronc rider had stopped him a few moments ago and given him an uncharacteristic—for a cowboy—hug. Then thanked him again and again.

"Just doin' my job, ma'am," he said, putting on his best *aw, shucks* attitude and voice.

"Well, you went above and beyond. Finn said you guys are the unsung heroes of the rodeo, and I guess you proved that tonight."

Her praise warmed his heart and his smile grew as their gazes held. "That means a lot to me."

"I was glad I could witness it." She took a step closer and then stood up on tiptoe and brushed a kiss over his cheek. "Your reward."

Vic caught her by the hand as she drew back. "That means more to me than the hug I just got from the cowboy."

"He gave you a hug? Hmm. I didn't know that was an option," Lauren teased. Then her expression grew serious. "I'm so thankful you're okay. That cowboy was lucky to have you around."

"Walden was there, too."

"I know, but you were the one who put your life on the line."

Her approval and admiration did much for his self-esteem even as he tried to minimize what he had done.

"So, are you heading home?" she asked as the horses in the trailer expressed their impatience by hitting their hooves on the aluminum sides.

"Yeah. I should get them out on pasture. And fed good for tomorrow."

"Well, I hope it goes well for you tomorrow."

"It would go even better if you agreed to go out with me tomorrow night."

She hesitated, and for a beat he thought he had misread her, pushed too far. Then she smiled and nodded. "That would be lovely."

"I thought we could go to Mercy. There's a new restaurant there, not too city, not too country. A good mix of both."

"So…champagne with the burgers," she said.

"Or soda with the oysters," he countered.

Her resounding laughter was like a cool breeze that washed over him.

"Great. I'll come by about five thirty to pick you up. If that's okay?"

"More than okay," she replied.

He touched her cheek with his finger, then swooped in and stole a quick kiss.

The flush on Lauren's cheeks was encouraging and adorable at the same time. He hadn't thought he could have that affect on her.

"I'll see you tomorrow," she said, her voice husky, her smile coy.

Then she walked away from him, but just before she turned down the alleyway where Jodie and Finn were, she shot a glance over her shoulder.

And gave him a smile that dived straight into his soul.

"Are you sure you don't want dessert?" Vic asked, reaching across the table of the restaurant and taking Lauren's hand.

She liked the casualness of it. The give-and-take of a comfortable relationship.

The restaurant was quiet for a Saturday evening, and she and Vic were tucked away in one corner. The lights were low, the music soft and candlelight cast Vic's chiseled features into shadow.

"I'm delightfully full," she said with a touch of regret as she glanced at the dessert menu lying beside her. "Though I have to say the pavlova cake and the lemon tart are tempting."

"We could split them?"

Lauren thought a moment, then shook her head. "No, thanks, but I will have some more coffee."

She wasn't ready to leave yet, to go back home and end this magical evening. At the ranch she was always reminded of what he might gain or lose and what was at stake for her and her future.

Here it was just her and Vic, with no decisions hanging over her head. She had shut her phone off to stop the increasing flurry of texts from Amy. She didn't want to think about anything but Vic.

"So Jodie was telling me that you might be doing the flowers for her wedding?" he asked.

"I might help out Aunt Laura."

"You girls used to work with your aunt in her shop, didn't you?"

"Mostly it was just me. Erin often had her nose buried in a book and Jodie would be upstairs in my aunt's apartment above the shop, plunking away on the piano."

Vic still held her hand, his fingers caressing hers. "That sounds great."

"My aunt's place was a small refuge for us. A place we could relax and be ourselves.

Being at her flower shop brought back some wonderful memories."

"Any other good memories of being here?" Vic asked.

Lauren twisted her fingers around his, looking down at them as she combed through her thoughts. "I remember going for trail rides up into the hills with Dad a few times. He could be patient when he chose to be." She looked up at him. "Going riding with you on the ranch brought back some of those memories. Reminded me of how beautiful the ranch is."

"So it wasn't always horrible to come here every summer?"

A peculiar tone had entered his voice. As if he needed to know how she felt about being here.

"No. It wasn't. In fact, we had a freedom here that we never had at our grandmother's place. Dad would give us a list of chores to do and then either go off to work or do other things on the ranch. Once we were done with our list, we could do our own thing. A benign neglect at times, but I think he didn't know what to do with three young girls all summer. Sometimes the chores took longer than we wanted them to and occasionally, if we rushed through them, he would make us do them over again if we didn't do them properly."

"What kind of chores did you have to do?"

"Believe it or not, we had chickens. Had to gather the eggs. Brush and groom the horses. Put halters on them and lead them around to get them used to being handled. Clean the house. Do laundry. Weed the flower beds, but that fell mostly to me. Jodie had to practice her piano. Erin was usually in charge of making supper. She was the better cook." Lauren's mind sifted back to that time, old memories coming out of being on her own with her sisters, laughing and joking and teasing each other. And, to her surprise, they made her smile. Then she turned her attention back to him. "What kind of chores did you have to do?"

"I can tell you Dean and I had it much tougher than you did," Vic said, his fingers making light circles on hers. "We had heavy-duty chores. Hauling and stacking square hay bales, moving large round ones. Helping move cows. Tractor work. Some field work. Manly stuff."

Lauren laughed at his mock seriousness. "Are you and Dean close? Finn told me that when he lived with you after his father died that he loved being at your parents' place."

Vic's expression grew pensive, then he gave her a wry smile. "Dean and I were close. Until…" His sentence faded away and a pained look crossed his features.

"Until the accident?" she prompted.

"Partly. But mostly until Tiffany."

She'd heard about her from Finn and Jodie. Now she wanted to know more.

"Who was she?"

"A girlfriend we had in common." He pulled his hand away, crossing his arms over his chest, his body language fairly crying out *no trespassing.*

But Lauren sensed that things were changing between her and Vic. She couldn't let this go. She felt as if they were on the cusp of something important. And she wanted to know everything about him before she dared move forward.

"What do you mean?"

"I'd liked her, and we dated for a while. But she was more attracted to Dean. So we broke up and she dated Dean for a couple of years," he said. "But then things weren't working out for them. Dean found out that she wanted to go out with me again. She didn't like the life Dean was living. Partying, drinking. You know what he was like."

She did. Dean always drove the fastest,

partied the hardest and talked the toughest. Those were many of the reasons why they'd talked Erin out of dating him when he'd asked her out years ago.

"Anyway, she got tired of it, so she said. She came to talk to me about him and in the process told me that it was me she really cared for. That dating Dean was a mistake." Vic sighed and shook his head. "I told her that she had to end it with Dean. That it wasn't fair to him. So she did. Trouble was, she told me she had done it the week before. So the night of the rodeo, she called me. Told me she was going to be in the audience. Watching me."

He shook his head. "Dean's horse was taking a while to settle down and I kept looking for her in the stands. Then I heard her call out to me. I turned to look at her just as Dean's horse jumped out of the chute. It was in that distracted moment that Dean was injured."

"What happened?"

"He made a turn away from where I was. His horse made a spin, not a bad one. Nothing Dean couldn't have handled, but for some reason Dean lost his balance. His leg was crushed against the fence and caught between the bars as the horse pulled away."

Lauren winced, thinking of how close some of today's riders had come to the fence.

"So you've always thought Dean's injury was your fault?"

"I should have paid attention. I shouldn't have looked when Tiffany called me."

Lauren heard the pain in his voice. The regret. Then something Vic had said caught her attention. "But you just said Dean could have handled the spin his horse gave him."

"It's not my job to assume that. It's my job to watch out for the cowboys. Always. And what made it worse was that Tiffany lied to me. She hadn't broken up with Dean the week before. She had just broken up with him that night. Right before he had to ride."

"How cruel of her."

"Not the best timing, but then, neither was mine."

"So in reality, Dean was even more distracted than you were," Lauren said.

"What are you saying?"

"Dean's frame of mine was probably worse than yours when he climbed on that horse. Just before he's supposed to ride, his girlfriend breaks up with him? He surely can't have had all his attention on what he had to do."

"Doesn't excuse my carelessness."

"Maybe not, but Dean's concentration should have been on his ride. I'm sure it wasn't. So most likely he wasn't performing the way he usually did. Even if you had been watching him the entire time, I doubt you could have prevented his accident."

The puzzled look on Vic's face told Lauren that he might not have considered this possibility before.

"When I saw you working today, I saw a man who was in charge. A man who knew exactly what he was doing all the time. The way you handled that cowboy caught up in his stirrup showed skill and foresight. You know what you're doing, and I don't think that one moment of distraction was the problem."

"So you're thinking Dean is as much to blame as I am."

"I'm not thinking it's a matter of who's to blame. I'm thinking the whole mess is a series of circumstances that were beyond your and Dean's control. It was an accident."

Vic sat back, frowning, as if mulling it over.

"I have a feeling that you and I are more alike than we realize," she continued. "I often felt guilty over what happened to Jodie— when she and Dad got into that awful fight and she injured her hand. I felt I should have been there to talk reason into both of them.

But I wasn't and I doubt I could have. I think as oldest siblings we feel like we have to take care of our younger sibs. And if something happens, we think it's our fault."

"Maybe."

He didn't sound convinced.

She leaned forward, reaching out to him. "I don't think it's right of you to take all that on yourself. Tiffany doesn't sound like she's a real class act. No offense." She realized too late how catty and jealous that might sound.

A wry smile crawled across Vic's lips. "She wasn't the best choice for either Dean or me. My mother never liked her, which should have been my first clue."

"At any rate, I think you've been putting too much of the blame on your shoulders, when I don't think it belongs there."

Vic took both her hands in his. Squeezed them hard. "Thanks for saying that. I don't agree with you one hundred percent, but I appreciate the sentiment."

"It's not a sentiment. You're a good man and you take good care of your family. You can't let this one event that wasn't even your fault take all the good parts of you away." She squeezed his hands back.

Then, to her surprise and pleasure, Vic lifted her hands to his lips and pressed a kiss to each one. He gave her a tender smile, his eyes glowing in the low light. "I think it's time to ask for the check."

A small thrill shivered down Lauren's spine. "I think I agree with you."

A few minutes later they were walking out of the restaurant across the darkened parking lot. The sun had set and the overhead lights cast captivating shadows.

They got to his truck, but before he opened the door, Vic pulled her into his arms, his hand cradling the back of her head. "You're a special person, Lauren McCauley," he said, his voice all husky.

Lauren slipped her hands around his neck, her fingers tangling in his hair. Then they drew closer, their lips meeting in a warm, tender kiss.

They pulled back after a few moments, looking into each other's eyes.

"I'm glad we did this," Vic said. "Took some time for just the two of us."

"I think we'll have to do it again."

"Are you going to church tomorrow?" he asked.

"Yes." She smiled at the thought. "It's been a while since I've attended regularly, but I liked going last week."

"You mean you didn't always enjoy it?"

Lauren gave him a look of regret. "We went with my father because it was expected, which created some resentment."

"But you'll be coming tomorrow?"

"Yes. I will."

"Would you like to go out on a picnic? After church?"

"That sounds wonderful."

"Then it's a date."

Lauren smiled at him and contentedly laid her head on his shoulder, her arm slipping around him as she held him close. This felt so right, she thought, her head resting on the warmth of his chest, possibilities dancing through her mind. Tentative plans. Hopeful dreams.

You thought the same about Harvey. And you were engaged to him for four years. Can you trust this guy?

The insidious voice was like a serpent, wriggling into the moment. Lauren tried to ignore it, but she couldn't get rid of it completely. And as she drew back, looking into Vic's face, she felt torn. Confused.

Emotions she didn't want in her life.

Certainty and solidity. That's what she was looking for.

Could Vic give that to her?

She wished she could be sure.

Chapter Eleven

"That was delicious," Lauren said, wiping her mouth with her napkin, then folding it up and setting it on the paper plate.

"You do realize that'll get thrown away," Vic teased her, leaning back on one elbow beside her. He twirled a blade of grass between his fingers, a feeling of utter contentment washing over him.

They had come back to his place after church and he had packed up the truck and driven to a spot where he, his father, Dean and Finn used to go.

Few people knew about it, even though it was on Bureau of Land Management land. He wanted Lauren to see it. To fall in love with the land.

To change her mind about leaving?

He realized that if he were honest with

himself, that was part of his reason. The other was he simply wanted to share with her something he enjoyed so much. To give her a small gift of peace.

"Force of habit," she said, brushing her hair back from her face as she continued tidying up.

Vic let her work, watching her, enjoying this small taste of domesticity. She had taken off the gray blazer she had worn to church; the scarf she had around her neck lay in a silky puddle on top of it. The simple blue T-shirt she wore enhanced the blue of her eyes, and her jeans were a surprisingly casual touch.

"Oldest-child syndrome," he teased, reaching over and running the blade of grass down her arm.

"Something you're not suffering from right now."

"I never had to do the dishes. Woman's work."

She grabbed the napkin package and bopped him on the head with it. He sat up, caught her arm and pulled him to her, dropping a kiss on her lips.

"You're not playing fair," she said.

"I didn't know we were playing a game," he returned, slipping his fingers through her hair.

"All of life is a game," she intoned in a mock-serious voice.

"And it doesn't matter if you win or lose—"

"It's how you play the game," she finished for him. "I wish more people played by the rules."

Her comment came from nowhere and he wanted to challenge her on it. But she pulled away and put the garbage into a bag, then set it in the cooler they had packed the lunch in.

"Now that you're done," he said, getting to his feet, "I have something I want to show you."

Lauren sat on her haunches, her head tilted to one side. "That sounds intriguing."

"Come with me." He held out his hand and she gave him a coy smile.

"Can I trust you?" she teased him.

He thought of what Jodie had told him. About her ex-fiancé.

And he grew suddenly serious.

"Always," he said.

Her expression softened and her eyes were intent.

"You know, I believe I can." She put her hand out and he pulled her up.

Vic led her out of the clearing over a narrow, worn path. Tree branches slapped at them and he pushed them aside best he could.

A few bugs followed, buzzing around their head. That, the faint rushing of water and their footfalls on the packed dirt were the only sounds in the stillness surrounding them.

"I can't get over how quiet it is up here," Lauren said, her voice lowered as if in reverence.

"I don't imagine you have much quiet living in the city."

"No. I didn't."

"Do you miss it yet? City living?"

She didn't reply and he glanced back again to catch her looking at him. "No. I haven't." Then she gave him a smile, and the glimmer of hope that had been ignited when she sat down beside him in church this morning grew.

He wanted to ask if she would consider staying in Montana, but he was afraid to hear her answer.

They eased down the narrow trail and then, as the sound of rushing water grew louder, he led her out onto a large, flat rock. Droplets of moisture from the water tumbling down over large boulders cooled the air, the water it fell into roiling from the force. But then as it flowed away from them, it settled into a quiet, deeper pool.

"This looks like something out of a movie," Lauren breathed, clinging to his hand.

"I spent a lot of happy times here," he said. She hugged her knees, looking pensive.

"What are you thinking about?" he asked, sitting down beside her.

"I was just remembering today's sermon. How hard it can be to trust God and, even more, people, when trust has been broken."

"Are you thinking of your fiancé?"

"Very much *ex*-fiancé," she corrected, looking at him. "And not only him, but other men in my life."

Vic felt a shiver of apprehension, but at the same time sensed they were slowly moving themselves to a place of trust. Much as he didn't like to think of her with other guys, this had been her reality.

"I've heard the verse that Pastor Dykstra preached on before," she said, resting her chin on her upraised knees. "But it seemed to hit home today."

"'Trust in the Lord with all your heart and lean not on your own understanding,'" Vic quoted from Proverbs.

"I've spent a lot of my life leaning on my own understanding," Lauren said, her voice growing quiet, contemplative. "I always fig-

ured I was the one who had to be in charge."
She turned her head toward him, giving him
a wry smile. "Always had a hard time accepting help, let alone asking for it."

"I got that from the first moment we met."

She granted him an apologetic smile. "I'm
sorry about that. I was feeling uptight. Tend
to feel that way around guys I'm attracted to."

"That sounds encouraging."

She grew serious again. "Harvey did a real
number on me—you may as well know that.
I was going to marry him. I had made a huge
commitment to him. And he broke that trust."

"Did he give you a reason for the breakup?"

Lauren released a harsh laugh. "He said
he'd never really loved me. And, looking
back, I believe that."

"Did you love him?" As soon as he spoke,
he wished he could take the words back. He
wasn't sure he wanted to know if she had.
But more importantly, it wasn't his business.

*But it is your business. You care for her.
You need to know what she's dealing with.*

"I thought I did. At first." Her quiet words
rested lightly in the air. "We were supposed to
be business partners. And I think it got hard
to separate the two relationships toward the
end. We spent more time arguing about busi-

ness than we did talking about wedding plans.
I think I knew the truth, but I was too afraid to
act on it. I figured he was my only chance. He
was my first boyfriend. I'd never dated much
before that. I didn't think you could break up
with a boyfriend, let alone a fiancé. I took the
idea of being faithful very, very seriously."

"I have a hard time believing he was your
only boyfriend," he said, brushing his fingers
over her knuckles.

"It's true. I was kind of uptight and smart
and nerdy, and I took on the burden of caring
for my sisters and grandmother. I was always
mature for my age, and I think guys didn't
know what to do with that," she said with a
light shrug.

He leaned in and gave her a kiss. Then another. "Then I have a lot to make up for, don't
I?"

Her eyes crinkled at the corners as she
smiled. "You're a special guy, Vic Moore."

Her comment was both encouraging and, if
he were honest, not precisely what he hoped
to hear.

Vic felt the precariousness of his own
changing feelings. She was growing more
and more important to him.

And he wanted her to know that.

So he kissed her again.

* * *

A shiver trickled down Lauren's spine as Vic's lips slowly left hers. Her lips grew cool and she wanted to kiss him again.

But she felt a warning niggling at her.

Men don't put your needs first.

Even as she looked into Vic's eyes, part of her sensed that this man was different.

She glanced down at her watch. She had promised Amy she would call her this afternoon. They needed to talk. Her plans for the future, which were once rock solid, had been shaken up by this man sitting next to her.

And she wasn't sure what to do about it.

"Do you need to go?" Vic asked.

"Sorry. I have to make a few phone calls this afternoon."

"Of course." He gave her a careful smile and she wondered if he sensed what those phone calls would be about.

He got up and started walking toward the path. She hesitated, looking at the pool, how restful it was, and yet it was a result of the turbulence of the waterfall.

Please, Lord, she prayed, *let me find my own place of rest. Help me to trust that You will watch over me and bring me where I should be.*

The drive back to the ranch was silent. As if each of them was lost in their own thoughts.

But all the way there, Vic held her hand. They exchanged the occasional glance, reinforcing what was growing between them.

She couldn't pass it off or ignore it anymore.

But she wasn't ready to face it head-on, either. The thought of putting her life into any man's hands… It made her tremble inside.

Lean not on your own understanding.

Could she trust God and believe, as the passage said, that He would direct her paths?

The thought of changing everything created a mixture of fear. But behind that lay an excitement and expectation she couldn't deny.

But which one would win out? She was taking charge of her own life with this new business venture.

Was it worth it?

The question seemed to rock her crumbling certainty.

Help me, Lord, she prayed. *I truly don't know what to do.*

"You okay?" Vic asked as he parked the truck beside her car. "You seem…pensive."

"That's a sensitive word for such a manly cowboy like you," she teased, taking refuge in humor. Deflecting and retrenching.

"I know how to use the thesaurus app on my phone," he said, his own tone light. Breezy.

She was comfortable with him in a way she'd never been with Harvey. And it was that, combined with her changing feelings for him, that was creating so much confusion in her life.

They got out of the truck. Lauren grabbed the blanket and Vic took the cooler. As they carried them up the walk to the house, Lauren looked past it to the corrals beyond.

"Is that Dean?" she asked.

Vic turned in the direction she was pointing, then abruptly stopped.

"That idiot is trying to get on that horse," he said, dropping the cooler on the sidewalk. "He hasn't tried to mount one on his own yet."

Lauren set the blanket down on the cooler and followed Vic as he jogged around the house. He skirted the edge of his mother's garden at the back of the house and headed to the corrals.

Just as Vic thought, Dean stood beside a horse that had already been saddled. His crutches leaned against the fence.

"Dean. Stop. Don't," Vic called out as he came closer.

Dean ignored him and, hobbling alongside the horse, led him to a box that stood by the fence.

"Let me help you," Vic said, climbing over the fence.

"Leave me alone," Dean called out. "I have to do this."

Vic walked over to Dean just as Dean struggled to get on top of the box. The horse shifted away from Dean, turning his head as if to see what was happening.

"You're distracting the horse," Dean called out.

Lauren heard the anger in his voice. And something else she couldn't identify. She was tempted to tell Vic to leave Dean alone, but she could also see from the way the horse was shifting around that Dean would need Vic's help.

Vic caught the halter rope and, moving closer to the horse, managed to get it to move sideways.

"You can probably get on now," Vic was saying.

But Dean didn't move.

"Dean?" Vic said, frowning at his brother.

"Why do you always think you have to take care of me? Why are you always fixing everything?"

Dean carefully stepped off the box and tossed Vic the reins. "I don't feel like riding now."

"But it would be so good for you," Vic said. "I think it's great that you want to go riding. I can help you make it happen."

Dean grabbed his crutches and fitted them under his arms. "I'm sure you can. But I need to do this on my own." He shot Vic an angry look. "There are some things in life you just can't fix."

He limped through the gate, then past Lauren. He gave her a cursory look, added a tight nod and headed toward the house.

Vic patted the horse on the side and, without another word, turned it around and tied it back up. With quick, sure movements he undid the cinches, slipping the saddle and blanket off the horse in one movement.

A few moments later the horse was unbridled and released. It shook its head, then moved to the middle of the pen, lowered itself to the ground and then, with awkward and ungainly movements, began to roll.

In spite of the tension that still shivered through the air, Lauren had to smile at the undignified sight.

And, thankfully, so did Vic when he came back from the tack shed.

"You goof," Vic said to the horse as he walked past it to open the gate. "You didn't even get sweated up."

"I've always wondered why they do that," Lauren said as Vic returned to her and climbed over the fence. It seemed easier to discuss the horse than to address what had happened between him and his brother.

"It's like scratching your back," Vic said. "Feels good."

The horse stood, shook off the dust, tossed its head at them and trotted off through the open gate to join the other horses.

Vic watched it a moment, his hands resting on the fence, then he looked over at Lauren. "Sorry about that. About Dean. I think he's just…frustrated."

Lauren nodded, acknowledging his comment but wondering if maybe Dean was right. She recognized the need to help. To jump in and try to fix. She had done it many times with her own sisters.

"You look like you'd like to say something more," he said.

He was too astute.

"It's okay," he prompted. "I've got thick skin."

"I'm an older sister and I know what you're trying to do," she said, choosing her words with care. "And it's wonderful that you want to help him, but I think Dean was right. He needed to do this on his own."

"He would have fallen and hurt himself," Vic said. "He's been doing so well with his rehab, I didn't want to see him lose all his progress with one stupid mistake."

"He was being careful," Lauren said. "He's a big boy."

"But what if…" Vic shook his head as if he understood what he was doing.

"What if he fell? He would get hurt. But I don't think he wanted to fall, so I doubt he would have taken any huge risk." Lauren stopped herself, realizing she was lecturing him.

Vic seemed to consider her comment. "I think you're right. I'm going to have to learn to leave things be with him."

Lauren laid her hand on his arm and gave a gentle squeeze. "Remember, it's not your fault, what happened to him. You don't have to work overtime to make up for it."

Vic gave her a grateful glance. "I suppose," he said. He cupped her face in his hand and she thought he was about to give her a kiss when her cell phone rang.

She looked down at the screen and her smile faded away.

It was Amy.

"I better take this," she said, holding up the phone.

She touched the screen, accepting the call as she walked away from Vic. But as she lifted the phone to her ear she heard nothing. She was too late.

A momentary reprieve, she thought, noticing that a text message had come in while her phone was ringing.

It was from Alex Rossiter.

Events and decisions were crowding in on her. She needed to make choices soon.

But as she turned back to look at Vic, she knew she couldn't put off her decisions any longer.

Chapter Twelve

"So, how was your date?" Jodie asked as Lauren dropped onto the deck chairs Jodie and Finn had found tucked away in one of the garages.

From her seat Lauren could look over the flower beds that now held splashes of red and purple, yellow and blue.

There were buds on the lilies, and though Nadine at the greenhouse had told her to cut them off, she had kept the flowers on. Next year they would bloom even more.

Next year.

I want to be here next year.

"You've got your thinking face on. Was the date that bad?" Jodie sat up, dropping her bare feet onto the wooden deck with a thump, her blue eyes wide. "Don't tell me—"

"The date was fantastic, if you must know,

and that's all I'm going to tell you." Lauren held up her hand to forestall any further questions from her sister.

"So, what's making you look so serious?"

Lauren kicked her shoes off and tucked them under her, leaning back in the chair, her eyes sweeping over the yard. Beyond the barn she saw fields rising to hills rising to mountains, purple edged against a sky slowly turning pink as the sun set.

"It's beautiful here, isn't it?" she said.

"Yeah. It is." Jodie inhaled a deep breath, then blew it out. "And you're thinking of moving back to the city. Living the dream."

"I don't know if I've ever thought of it as the dream," Lauren said. "I think owning my own business with Amy was a means to an end."

"The end being independence."

"Sounds kind of empty now, doesn't it."

"It is. Independence is overrated. You can't tell me that you'd prefer to own your own business, live in an apartment downtown and head off to work in an office every day. Wearing high heels? Every day?"

Lauren chuckled at the disgust in her sister's voice. "I can wear flats, too."

"Is that what you want? Compared to

this?" Jodie swept her hand out, encompassing the view.

Lauren shook her head. She didn't.

"Then can't you stay?"

"I want to," she whispered, thinking of Vic and what they had shared. His love for his brother. His solidity. "But what would I do here? I wouldn't have my own life."

"I know that's important to you."

"You have your music, your composing. You have your own place and a future with Finn."

"You could start an accounting business here."

"Maybe. But I would have to start from scratch."

"Would you want to do it? For Vic?"

"The idea of making that kind of sacrifice for another man scares me to death. I did it with Harvey, and while I know Vic is nothing like Harvey…"

She let the sentence drift off, knowing that Vic was ten times the man Harvey was.

"I know exactly how this works," Jodie said, pulling her chair closer and taking Lauren's hand in hers. "Finn made me nervous, too. But I learned to trust him. Vic is a good guy. I know you can trust him."

Lauren nodded, her head doing battle with her heart.

"What's going on behind that cool, calm facade of yours?" Jodie pressed.

"Obligations. Promises. And the fact that what Amy and I are planning gives me control over my life."

"You know that none of us ever can control our lives," Jodie said. "I had to learn that lesson long ago. So many things come along that can toss over that particular apple cart."

Lauren heard the wisdom in her words.

"But here, in Saddlebank, you have a community you can be a part of. A church that's dynamic and welcoming. You have me and you have a man who, I believe, truly cares about you."

"Maybe," was all she said.

"I've seen a real change in you since you've come back," Jodie continued. "You seem more relaxed. Less uptight. You've lost that frown line between your eyebrows, and your mouth isn't as pinched. I've seen you smile more the past few weeks than I've seen in a long time."

"I am happier," she admitted, giving her sister one of those smiles that did come easier than they had before.

"And you look happier now than you did

with Harvey." Jodie gave her a pensive look. "I sometimes wonder if you really loved him."

"I've wondered the same thing." She toyed with her sister's engagement ring, turning it so it caught the sun, emitting sprinkles of light. She'd had a ring just like it. In her mind it represented success and security, but it had all been a lie. "I think Harvey became a habit after a while. It was easier to stay with him than to think about what my life would be like if I left him."

"And Vic? How do you feel about him?"

Lauren's heart turned over in her chest as thoughts of Vic overshadowed the vision of independence she'd carried with her since getting laid off.

"I care about him more than I want to think about," she said. "He makes me feel like I want to be a better person."

Her phone rang, and with a feeling of anticipation she reached for it. Vic had asked her to text him when she got home. Just to make sure she made it safely, he had said with a teasing grin.

But as she glanced at the screen, her heart dropped. It wasn't Vic. It was Amy.

"I've got to take this," she said as she got up. "I missed her last call. Please excuse me." But as she walked into the house, she realized that at one time texts and calls from Amy about their plans had created a sense of excitement.

Now they created a sense of dread.

"Well, I guess that's the last of it." Vic leaned back in the office chair, tamping down his fear as they set the file containing Keith's personal papers aside.

Though nothing had emerged from the last few times he was here, he'd felt an urgency to try one last time. The problem was now he wasn't only looking to protect his interests in the ranch—he was hoping to give Lauren a reason to stay.

After their last date, he felt even more strongly than before that Lauren belonged here. He just wished he could convince her of that.

"I'm sorry we couldn't find anything," Lauren said, reaching over and turning the computer off.

"Me, too." He glanced at his phone lying on the desk as the time registered. "And I gotta go. Dwayne is coming to pick up your dad's truck."

"It's still at your ranch?"

"Yeah. Since your father's accident."

He pushed up from his chair, fighting to resign himself to that reality. He held his hand out to her to help her up and she took it. She stood in front of him now and lifted one hand, resting it on his shoulder.

He studied her features, wondering what she would say if he asked her to stay, knowing that if he did, he was heading down a one-way path himself.

Because asking her to stay meant sticking his neck out.

The last time he had done that, with Tiffany, the results had been disastrous.

That wasn't your fault.

And yet, he felt as if his pushing Tiffany away had been the flashpoint that turned his and Dean's lives around.

He didn't want anything to happen with Lauren. He wanted her to decide for herself.

"You look like you've got heavy things on your mind," she said as her phone buzzed yet again.

It had been ringing all morning, but she'd ignored it. He knew things were coming to a head.

"Are you going to get that?"

She shook her head.

He fought down a sudden beat of frustration. "I'm sure Alex doesn't appreciate being strung along like this."

She gave a noncommittal nod.

"Are you going through with the ranch deal with Alex?"

"I don't know."

"What about us?"

"Us?" Her frown wasn't encouraging, and it didn't help his growing frustration, either.

"I thought there was an *us*. I though we were moving toward that."

"I think we are—"

"Think?" He took a step back, the words he wanted to speak clogging up his throat. "You *think* we are? After all what we've shared? I *know* we have something special."

The anger in his voice masked the fear that she was considering leaving.

"I did. I really did."

"Did." He pounced on that word. "So what happened? I thought we were creating a relationship, you and me."

"I'm sorry," was all she could manage.

His fear grew, which only stoked his anger more. "Sorry. What does that mean?"

"It means I'm sorry."

"For what? For spending time with me? For leading me on? For making me think that something was happening between us?"

He knew he should stop, but he rushed headlong, heedless, afraid.

Then he saw a spark of anger kindle in her eyes, saw her lips thin, her hands clench.

And he knew he had pushed her too hard.

His anger was a surprise and, at the same time, it ignited hers.

How dare he accuse her of leading him on?

She straightened to her full height. There was no way she was going to let him have the advantage of height, towering over her in his anger.

Though in spite of that, she still had to look up at him.

Still had to look up into those eyes, which only a few moments ago had looked at her with such affection, but now were narrowed in antagonism.

"I was never leading you on," she shot back, still trying to figure out how things had shifted so quickly.

"So something was happening between us."

"*Is* happening." The words slipped out and she could see from the way his expression shifted, he had caught it, as well.

"Then why is Alex still texting you? Why are you taking a job I'm sensing you feel obligated to? Is it the money?"

"That helps."

"So that's what this all comes down to?" He released a short laugh and her back stiffened.

"You know, it's so easy for you to judge me," she said, trying to keep her own rising emotions under control. "You have a mother who cares about you. People who you matter to you. You've probably never had to scrabble for your next dollar."

"I can't imagine you doing that," Vic said. "You've had a good job for many years. Don't tell me you haven't managed to save up."

In spite of her resolve, her anger grew. "Okay, I won't tell you how Harvey smiled at me, all the while bilking thousands out of the joint business account that took us years to set up. An account that he emptied in days. How I thought I trusted him and as soon as he had a choice between work and me, he chose work and he took our money. You know, he not only left me at the altar. He left me flat broke. It's not something I'm proud of. Not something I let anyone know. I'm supposed to be so smart, so good with money, and some lying, sneaky…man took everything from me. You talk about buying this place, and while I'd love to sell it to you, I told you that I can't afford to. I need every penny of it to pay for this business."

"Which you're still leaving to run."

How could she explain to him what this meant to her without making it look as though she wanted to leave him? She wanted the security and independence of her own business, but she wanted him, too.

But she couldn't have both. Choosing the business meant losing him. Choosing the ranch meant losing herself.

"What about Jodie? And Erin? You seem to be able to make your decisions in your own little world."

"Because that's what I learned," she shot back. "All my life I've had to be in charge. When we left this ranch, my mother was a wreck. We moved into my grandmother's house on sufferance. I had to take care of my sisters because my grandmother barely tolerated us. After my mother died, even more so. We were shunted here in the summer to give my grandmother a break. My father didn't know what to do with us so, once again I was in charge. When my grandmother got sick, guess who took care of her? Even Harvey required sacrifices from me. Saving money so we could build up our business and our future together. I've given everything I have to give to everyone I've ever known."

Her voice caught as the humiliation of that

crashed in on her again. But she wasn't going to let that determine her future. "All of my life it's been about other people. Taking care of everyone else. Watching out for everyone else."

She drew in a slow breath, her anger slowly easing out of her. "Just for once, I'd like to think of me. Make a decision for me."

Though he held her angry gaze, his own eyes narrowed, she sensed a shifting in his attitude. As if he was at least considering what she had to say.

And just then a muffled ringtone sounded in the office.

She pulled her cell phone out of her back pocket and glanced at it with a sigh of resignation. "It's Alex."

"Of course it is." Vic drew back, and anything she thought she'd seen there was replaced with an icy stare. "Then I better go."

He gave her a curt nod, grabbed his hat and dropped it on his head as he spun on his heel.

Then he left.

Chapter Thirteen

"Hey, Alex, what can I do for you?" Lauren said, wearily dropping into her father's office chair. Her hands were still trembling from her fight with Vic.

How had things gone so badly so quickly?

He was pushing her. He wanted a decision and she wasn't ready to give it to him.

She pressed her fingers against her temple.

"You've been hard to get hold of," he said. "You sure you still want to do this deal? 'Cause you seem to be less than enthusiastic." He sounded testy and Lauren wondered if he would back out. The idea created a sliver of fear. But behind that was a surprising sense of relief. If Alex didn't buy the ranch…

Amy would be left hanging. And her own plans would change. Everything she'd been working toward would disappear. Swept out of her life.

She thought back to the fight she'd just had with Vic. The angry words she'd thrown at him.

How she'd told him things she'd never wanted to reveal.

He had goaded her into it, she told herself. Pushed her into a corner.

"I still want to make this happen," she said. "But I'm curious, would you run it as a ranch? Would you be willing to lease it to Vic?"

"I could care less one way or the other. To tell you the truth, buying the ranch is just a way to dump some money," Alex said. "More of an investment for me than anything."

An investment. Jodie's words about Alex returned and Lauren wondered why it mattered.

But it did. Vic had long-term plans for this place. He would nurture it. It was part of the Saddlebank legacy. Refuge Ranch had just celebrated 150 years of continuous ownership. That was a huge feat in this day and age. There was history in this place, she thought, leaning her elbows on the desk, looking out the window over the land that had been cared for and nurtured for generations of her father's family.

And your family.

"Anyhow, gotta run," Alex said. "My people will talk to your people in the next few days." And before she could say anything, he hung up. Off to another business meeting, amassing more money to invest in other properties.

Then she had something else that needed her attention, because her phone had beeped while she was talking to Vic.

Amy. Sending another text. Wondering what was going on.

The pressure of other people's expectations dragged her in so many directions. Vic. Alex. Amy.

Maybe she should let Vic purchase the ranch. Maybe she and Amy could make a lesser offer on the business. Get creative about financing for the rest.

So you can move to the city and live the dream?

The thought, once so enticing, now seemed empty and depressing.

As the thought of leaving Vic, of not having him in her life, registered, she felt a sharp, dull pain beneath her breastbone. Sharper than any pain Harvey had ever dealt her.

She closed her eyes, pressing her hands to her face.

Help me to trust, Lord. Help me to know what to do. Help me to see You as my all in all.

The passage from Sunday alighted into her mind.

Trust in the Lord... He will direct your paths.

But the thought of letting go of all her plans still spooked her. Made her feel untethered. Lost. She had hitched her wagon to other men's stars before and had been left hanging. Been disappointed.

Vic is not Harvey. He's not your father.

Confused and frightened, she grabbed her phone and dialed Amy's number.

"Thank goodness you called, girlfriend," Amy said, breathless. "I've been getting all panicky. The sellers have been putting major pressure on me. How are things progressing on the sale?"

"I just talked to Alex. He still wants to go ahead."

"That's great news. Did he give you a date for closing the deal? We're going to need those funds soon."

"No. I have to talk to my lawyer." She let her eyes scan over the land. "I just wish Alex didn't see it as only an investment. I wish he wanted to see it run as a working ranch."

"What do you care about that?" Amy asked. "You just want the money."

Did she? Really? Was the ranch that disposable to her?

Once again she wished she could talk to Erin. Really talk to her. Not just terse text messages. Find out where she was. But the last phone call she'd had with Erin was a brief conversation about how things were going. Erin hadn't wanted to know about the ranch. She'd just said that she'd be fine with whatever they decided.

And while Lauren knew how Jodie felt, she had been surprisingly supportive.

"Speaking of money, do you think the sellers would take a lesser offer?" she asked, floating the idea. "I was thinking we could talk to the bank and increase our long-term loan."

"Why are you talking about this at the last minute?" Amy said. "You know we went over and over this. We'll need every penny from the sale of the ranch to add to what I've got to make this work. The bank will only carry us for so much. And that's thanks to your credit rating."

Lauren once again felt the sting of Harvey's betrayal. The disgrace of having her credit rating go from stellar to ugly with a few swipes of an already overcharged credit card that he had neglected to tell her about. A card in both their names that he had maxed out and then left her responsible for.

"You can't back out now, friend," Amy warned. "You just can't. You know how much this means to me."

"I'm not backing out. It's just…"

"You've been sounding weird the last few calls," Amy said. "Is there something going on that I need to know about?"

Vic, Lauren thought, pressing her fingers against her temples. Vic's need to take this ranch on.

"You're not thinking of backing out, are you?"

Lauren hesitated.

"You know you owe me, Lauren."

And there it was. The card that Amy had said she would never play. The debt was finally getting called in.

"I know." Lauren was quiet, thinking of those darker days. After Harvey had left her and she'd had less than nothing, Amy had taken her in. Had given her a place to live and told her it didn't matter that she was unable to make rent. Jodie had been dealing with her own stuff and was unable to help out. And she couldn't go to Erin.

But Amy had been there every step of the way, letting her stay while Lauren paid off the credit-card debt Harvey had left her with.

Though she'd managed to repay Amy most everything, she could never repay her kindness. Now the piper needed to be paid, Lauren thought.

"This isn't because of this guy, is it?" Amy asked. "This guy who wants to buy the ranch instead of Alex?"

Lauren's wants and needs fought with each other in her head. "He's got good plans for this place. He wants to buy it for his brother."

"Are you falling for this guy?" Amy said, a faintly accusing tone in her voice.

Lauren wanted to deny it, but she couldn't. Because she knew she was past that point. In spite of the angry words they had traded just a few moments ago, she knew she was far more connected to Vic than she wanted to admit.

The anger he had thrown at her hurt. If he hadn't mattered, his words couldn't have wounded her so deeply.

"Girlfriend, do I need to remind you of how lost you were after Harvey dumped you? How I would listen to you talk about your dad? And your last boss? You know what they all have in common? They're guys. And you know better than anyone that you have to take care of yourself. That you can't count on a guy to do that for you."

Her words flew at Lauren, striking with deadly accuracy, resurrecting insecurities that still hounded her.

"I know I do. And you know how grateful I am to you for everything." Still she hesitated, torn by her conflicting desires.

I thought we were moving to an us.

Her heart stuttered as his words resonated in her mind.

She pressed on. "Please talk to the bank anyhow. See if they can work with the numbers I'm going to text you. Just float it past them."

"Okay. Just so you know, if they decline, we're still a go, correct?"

"I understand."

"Stay the course," Amy reminded her, repeating words that Lauren had often lobbed her way when they were making these plans. "No guy is worth sacrificing your independence for."

They said goodbye, then Lauren tossed her cell phone on the desk, spinning her chair around, a reflection of her own mind.

Stay the course. No guy is worth it.

She pushed herself out of her chair. She needed to get out of here. To think.

She strode out of the house, got in her car and headed out. She didn't know where she was going. The only thing she knew was that she had to get away.

Clear her head.

What had he done?

Vic slammed his hand on the steering wheel, frustrated and furious with himself.

He always prided himself on being even-keeled and steady. The sudden flashes of anger and fury had always belonged to Dean.

But this?

He groaned aloud as he relived the things he had said to Lauren. The pain he might have caused.

It was fear that drove him to it, he told himself. Fear that things were coming to a head.

Fear that he would lose Lauren.

He wanted to call her and apologize.

For what?

Telling her how he felt? Laying out what he had hoped was happening?

Unconsciously he reached in his pocket to get his cell phone.

But his pocket was empty. He dug in his other shirt pocket, then he remembered. The last time he had used his phone was in Keith's office at the Circle M Ranch. He must have left it there. He stopped the truck and drew in a deep breath.

Though he didn't want to go back, maybe this was a chance to make amends for his behavior.

He turned the truck around, gunned it and headed back.

Lauren's car was gone when he arrived, which gave him a mixture of relief and regret.

No second chances here.

And though he knew no one was home, he still knocked on the door, then he stepped into the house, an echoing silence greeting him. Then he heard a faint ding.

Notification that a text message was coming in on his phone. Probably Dwayne telling him when he was coming to pick up Keith's truck. He followed the sound back to the office and saw his phone sitting on the desk beside the computer, the screen lit up with the message.

Echoes of the fight he and Lauren had had lingered. Words he wished he could take back hovered. And in spite of that, part of him still clung to the hope that Lauren wanted to stay.

He shook them off, grabbed his phone and swiped across the screen to read the text.

Deal is a go. Terms as originally planned. Excited to start working together. Here's to a future free from men.

He glanced at the sender, confused. Someone named Amy.

As he read it again, the puzzling words finally registered. As did the fact that the screen on this phone was pristine. His was scratched with a small crack in the corner.

He was holding Lauren's phone. And this text had come from the partner Lauren was going into business with.

Lauren was going through with the sale.

That was it. It was over. Done.

He put the phone down and as he did, he saw his own phone, half-hidden under a stack of papers. He pulled it out and shoved it in his back pocket, waves of sorrow and anger rising up in him.

Lauren was leaving.

He strode out of the house toward his truck, got in and drove back toward his place, his heart heavy in his chest.

He didn't want to think about it but couldn't stop.

He wanted to pray but didn't know what to

pray for. As he drove, he stared at the road stretching ahead of him. Empty. Lonely.

Stop writing country songs. Get a grip. She's just a woman.

But she wasn't just a woman. She was Lauren. And corny as it sounded, he knew that her leaving would create an emptiness in his life he didn't know he could ever fill.

Help me through this, Lord, he prayed. *Give me strength to deal. Help me to lean on You. Not on my own understanding.*

Pulling in a deep breath, he felt his emotions steady, his anger and exasperation with himself and with Lauren push to the back of his mind.

At the same time, the words she'd thrown out rose up again.

Just for once I'd like to think of me.

Coming from someone else, that could have sounded selfish. But even before he met Lauren, he had heard Jodie say how selfless her sister was. How she had done so much for her and Erin.

Lauren's admission about Harvey added another layer.

But behind that came his own reality. It was time to tell Dean that it was over.

And as he turned his truck into the driveway of the ranch, he felt his heart sink at the thought.

Then he saw Dwayne's tow truck, parked by the barn. He had other things to deal with. Vic hopped out of his truck, to give Dwayne directions where to go.

Vic had pulled Keith's truck back behind the hay barn after the accident and hadn't looked at it since. He couldn't. Each time he saw the busted-in window and the crumpled cab, he thought of Keith. He was thankful that he had put it where it was so Lauren hadn't had to see it the few times she had come to his place.

His stomach twisted at the thought of Lauren.

The ranch would be sold to an absentee owner. Another ranch become victim of wretched excess.

And the worst part of this was that it meant Lauren was leaving. He had shown her what he could and told her what he dared. And she was still going.

Help me to let go, Lord, he prayed. *Help me to be happy for her. To know that if this is what she wants, then this is good.*

But even as he prayed, he couldn't rid himself of the idea that maybe this wasn't entirely what she wanted. But he had to let go. Let her do whatever it was she thought she wanted to do. Give her the space to do it.

"Did anyone come and get the registration papers from the truck?" Dwayne asked as he jumped out of the cab of his truck, ready to hook up the winch cable.

"Insurance company didn't need them. They had everything on file."

"I might need them. Just in case," Dwayne said, pulling on his gloves.

While he got ready, Vic walked over to the truck and yanked on the passenger door. It took a few tries, but he finally jerked it open. The glove box proved just as unwieldy. He pulled his jackknife out of his pocket and fiddled with the latch, then finally managed to get it open. The insurance papers and registration card were tucked in a black vinyl folder inside. He pulled the folder out and as he did a stained and wrinkled envelope came with it and drifted to the floor of the truck.

Vic bent over and picked it up. Then frowned.

The envelope had his name scrawled across the front. In Keith McCauley's handwriting.

A chill feathered down his spine as things came together. Keith McCauley had been on his way to Vic's place when he had his accident. Had he been coming to deliver this?

He thought of the letters Lauren and Jodie had mentioned. Letters that spoke of regrets and sorrow and offered apologies. Was this letter one of those?

"Got the stuff?" Dwayne asked as Vic slowly closed the door, still staring down at the envelope.

"Yeah. Here it is." He handed him the folder but folded up the letter and tucked it in the back pocket of his blue jeans.

Dwayne flipped open the folder and shot Vic a puzzled glance. "You look kinda pale. You okay?"

"I'm fine. Let's get this truck loaded up and out of here."

Twenty minutes later the truck was on the flat deck, Dwayne was headed back to town and Vic was finally alone. He tugged the envelope out of his pocket, trudged over to the corrals and sank down on a hay bale. He held the letter a moment, thinking of Keith. Remembering.

Then he ripped opened the envelope and tugged out two pieces of paper.

The first was a letter.

Dear Vic,
I want you to know that I hope to get to the lawyer and do this right but for

now this note will have to do. We never signed anything permanent so until we do, I want you to have this. Keith.

Vic read over the letter once again, then set it aside and glanced quickly over the second piece of paper.

Across the top of the letter, Keith had written, "Lease Agreement Between Keith McCauley and Vic Moore."

Vic swallowed, and his heart did double time, pounding in his chest. This was the documentation he had been looking for all this time.

This document verifies that I, Keith McCauley, am leasing my ranch, the Circle M, to Vic Moore. This is a lease-to-own agreement.

Vic dragged his hand over his face and continued. The agreement went on to state that Keith agreed to sell Vic the Circle M Ranch for a set amount of money in the first year he leased it, then a set amount if he bought it in the second year.

Vic had leased it for three years, so the second number applied. And it was exactly the amount Keith and Vic had agreed upon.

The amount he had figured on when he spoke with Lauren at Drake's office the first time he saw her.

The amount that didn't come close to what Alex, the current buyer, was offering her.

He leaned back against the fence as the implications of this letter sank in.

He would have to talk to Drake. See if it was legitimate. But he guessed it would be as legal as the will Keith had drawn up in his own handwriting.

Would Lauren contest it?

She could stay now. Would have to. She couldn't buy the business if he exercised his rights to the ranch.

But was that what he wanted? To force her hand? He wanted her to choose of her own free will. He thought of what she had told him about her ex.

He could only imagine how humiliating it must have been not only to be dumped the week of her wedding but also to be so duped by a man you thought you were going to share your life with.

Just for once I'd like to think of me.

"Hey, honey, what's up?"

His mother's voice behind him made Vic jump. He spun around in time to see her walking toward him, her hat hanging to one side, as she pulled off her gardening gloves.

"I was working out in the garden and saw you sitting here. What's going on?" she asked, lowering herself to the bale beside him.

Vic wasn't sure he was ready to talk about what had happened, but he knew the facts would come out some time or other.

"I just found this in Keith's truck," he said, holding out the papers for his mother to look at. "It's the lease agreement I've been looking for all this time."

"You found it?" His mother took the papers and glanced over them, her eyes flying over the words. "All this time and they were right here. You could have saved yourself so much trouble."

And a broken heart.

His mother handed Vic the papers back. "Is something bothering you?"

Vic folded up the papers and slipped them back in the envelope. "This agreement means I can probably stop Lauren from selling the ranch to Alex." Vic turned to his mother and gave her a wan smile. "Which means I'll have dibs on the ranch. For Dean. It means I can finally take care of him."

"I know how much that means to you," she said, slipping her hat off her head. "But

I think you need to know that we never expected you to take care of Dean. I know that you seem to think it was your fault Dean got hurt. That you should have stopped it."

She gave Vic a caring look. "I don't think Dean ever expected you to take care of him. I know I certainly didn't, and I think it's time you let go of that notion."

Vic heard his mother on one level and understood, but months and months of thinking he had to take care of his brother were hard to shake.

"Maybe not. Maybe my reasons for buying Keith's ranch were tied up with him. But I still think it's a good opportunity."

"It is. And I'm sure Dean would be happy if you ended up with it. But I think it's time you make this decision for yourself. Not for Dean. You've taken on too much. You have to let Dean take care of himself. Live with the consequences of his own actions."

As Vic listened to his mother, he felt an easing of the burden he'd been carrying all this time. But at the same time, while one weight had fallen off his shoulders, it was as if another one had replaced it.

Now it was entirely up to him to decide what to do for his own reasons.

And as he thought of what Lauren had told

him and what the repercussions of this agreement would be for her, he knew exactly what he had to do.

Chapter Fourteen

"So I've kept my mouth shut for the past five minutes, but now you have to tell me about that sad face of yours," Aunt Laura said as she placed a delicate fern in the floral arrangement she was working on.

Fifteen minutes ago, two hours after she drove away from the ranch, Lauren had walked into her aunt's flower shop. As she stepped inside, a bell above the door tinkled. The muted drone of the refrigerated case holding an assortment of arrangements and the mixed scents of flowers, potpourri and candles enfolded her in a familiar embrace. Sighing with relief, Lauren had followed her aunt's tuneless humming to the back room, where Aunt Laura was perched on a stool at the butcher-block table. A huge mug of coffee was parked beside her and a glorious spill of flowers in front of her.

Lauren grinned as she sorted through the flowers she was working with. "I should have guessed you wouldn't miss that."

"I just know my girls," Aunt Laura said, twisting a red silk ribbon into a bow and tying some wire around it. "And as soon as you came into the shop, I knew something was wrong."

But, bless her aunt's heart, she didn't say anything. Didn't press. Just gave Lauren some flowers and directions and time.

Lauren snipped a rose, then carefully cut the thorns off before inserting it in the block of Oasis that would hold the arrangement. "It's been a bad morning," she said as she picked up a white lily and pared it down. She felt a quiver of sorrow rise up her throat and she swallowed it down. She didn't want to cry.

She had done enough of that on her drive around the county. She'd stopped at the lookout point and sat a moment, overlooking the valley and the Saddlebank River, letting the beauty wash over her. A love and appreciation for this place had been easing its way into her heart and soul ever since she arrived.

Looking out over the valley, she'd felt a sense of continuity from the only place in her life that had always been there. Had always been a part of her life.

And now someone else had found a place in her heart.

She had tried not to think of Vic, but every word they spoke, every emotion that had spilled out, washed over her again and again.

Thankfully she'd forgotten her phone at the ranch, so she didn't have to deal with Amy and Alex and their incessant demands.

But still her aunt said nothing.

"Vic and I had a fight," she said after a long pause.

"Oh, dear. That's not good." She didn't press for details.

But Lauren knew she needed to talk this through.

"It was about the ranch and the business I want to buy."

"What did you fight about?" Aunt Laura asked.

"I think he was hoping I would stay."

"Why would he hope that?"

Her aunt's comment seemed artless, but Lauren heard the other question behind that.

And why didn't you want that?

I do want it, she thought.

But Alex and Amy and expectations and dreams of independence clung with tentacles she was afraid to pull away from.

"Because we've been spending time together. Because we've..." Her voice faltered.

"We've?" her aunt said, her tone encouraging.

Lauren ripped a tiny strip off a banana leaf, twisting it around the flowers she arranged, the words rising up her throat, demanding to be articulated.

"We've kissed. We've shared dreams. We've talked about our faith," she said, her voice wavering with sudden and unwelcome emotion. But once she started it was as if the words rose up, needing to be spoken aloud. "We've spent enough time together that I dared to think I was able to let someone into my life again. But I've got all this other stuff going on and I can't sort it out. Alex. Amy. The business. My plans for the future."

She twisted up another leaf, inserting it in the arrangement. "Trouble is, I don't know if I want that anymore. I don't know what I want." She picked up another lily, catching her breath. "And yet my practical self, the part of me that helped me survive living with Gramma, taking care of my sisters, my mother, working my fingers to the bone so that Harvey and I could get set up and then getting dumped—that part of me tells me not to be foolish. To take care of me first."

Her aunt calmly snipped another carnation and placed it in the piece she was working on.

"That sounds serious," she said, not meeting Lauren's eyes.

Lauren was surprised at the relief she felt at finally being able to speak about what had been tangled up in her mind the past few hours.

"Do you care for Vic?" her aunt asked, finally looking directly at her.

Lauren held her gaze and then her shoulders slumped. "More than I want to admit. More than I've ever cared for anyone."

"If you could let go of expectations from other people and demands and old dreams you've clung to, if you could set them all aside and narrow everything down to you, what would you choose?"

"It's not that easy. Everything is so wound around everything else, I don't know how to untangle it."

"Have you prayed about this?"

Lauren split off another piece of the banana

leaf, turning it over in her hands, trying to do exactly what her aunt suggested.

"I'm not sure what to pray."

"I think you have to be careful not to expect that God will suddenly show up with a bolt of lightning and give you the answer. I think you have to acknowledge that you need to place your life in His hands and trust that the people He has placed in your life will also, if they are faithful, watch over you."

"Other than you, I don't know if that's ever happened."

Her aunt came to stand beside her, slipping her arm around Lauren's shoulders. "Ever since you were a little girl, you've always watched over your sisters. Always been watching out for someone else. I know that. I heard a saying once and I think you should try to apply it now. Sometimes the place where your head and your heart intersect is the place where your best decision is made. So think of where that happens. Think of what you want and what you need and see if there's a connection."

Lauren shot her aunt a puzzled glance as what she said seemed to settle. Take root.

"I think I just want something that belongs to me. A place and business of my own...but

I don't want to be on my own." She drew in a slow breath as a new realization grew. "I want to be with Vic. If everything else was stripped away, I'd want to be with him. But I'm afraid that if I do…"

"He'll have control over you."

Lauren nodded, surprised at her aunt's ability to see past the trees and identify the forest.

"That's something you'll have to deal with," her aunt continued. "Trust is a huge part of any relationship, and if you can't trust, then the foundation is weak." Aunt Laura squeezed just a little harder. "So my question to you is, can you trust Vic?"

"My heart tells me I can."

"And your head?"

Lauren thought of everything Vic was willing to do to secure the ranch for his brother. How he put up with her own initial antagonism. How regularly he showed up to go through papers and the computer, always hoping something would happen. All for his brother.

How attentive he could be. How caring.

"My head tells me that Vic is a good man. That he would take care of anyone in his life. And he has."

Lauren felt a flicker of fear even as she

spoke the words. The thought of what she could be leaving behind if she went through with her plans with Amy.

What she could lose.

Then the store's phone rang just as a bell above the entrance announced a new customer.

"You take care of your customer," Lauren said. "I'll get the phone."

"Floral Folly," she said, tucking the handset under her ear as she turned back to the arrangement she'd been working on.

"Finally," Jodie said, breathless. "I've been calling and calling your cell phone. I thought Aunt Laura might know where you are and here I get you. Where have you been?"

"I've been driving around," she said. She didn't want to talk to Jodie right now. Didn't want to talk about what Vic might have told Finn, who might have told Jodie.

"Have you talked to Vic?"

Nothing like coming directly to the point.

"When?" she asked, preferring to see where her sister was going before she blindly stumbled along behind her.

"In the last half hour or so?"

"No."

"Have you talked to Drake? He's been trying to call you, too."

"No. I haven't."

"You should call Drake. Then Vic."

"I don't feel like it right now."

"Well, then I'll let you know what happened. Are you sitting down?"

"Yes." A prickle of fear trickled down Lauren's neck. "It's not Erin, is it?"

"What? No. Not Erin. It's Vic. He went to see Drake. Apparently he found that lease agreement he was looking for. It laid out the terms of the lease and the buyout."

Lauren's heart rate, already increasing, now began pounding in earnest. She knew the buyout amount from the figure Vic had quoted her. And it was less than what Alex was willing to pay. "What does that mean? Is it legal?"

"Apparently. Dad signed it and Drake verified it."

Lauren swallowed, confusion warring with happiness for Vic and fighting with concern over how this would affect her.

"So, what do we do now?"

"Well, we don't do anything. Vic told Drake he wasn't following through on it. He didn't want to claim his legal rights to first purchaser of the ranch at the amount Dad had written in the agreement."

Lauren struggled to keep up with the words her sister was breathlessly tossing at her.

"What?"

"Vic has the lease agreement. It's legal. But he's not exercising his rights of first refusal," Jodie said again. "You do know what this means, doesn't it?"

Lauren still wasn't sure. Her head was spinning as she tried to absorb this startling turn of events.

"Where did he find it?"

"Apparently in the glove box in Dad's truck. He was driving to Vic's place when… when he rolled the truck." Jodie stopped there, her voice breaking just a little.

Lauren felt as if her brain was exploding with all the information she'd just heard.

"So he brought the agreement to Drake?"

"Yeah. To have it verified, I guess. And then he changed his mind."

"Did Drake say why?"

"Nope. You'll have to talk to him."

That was going to be her next call.

"So nothing's changed, has it?" Jodie said, her voice rising with a faint note of hope that begged Lauren to negate what she had just said.

"I don't know what to think," Lauren said truthfully. "I can't believe he did this."

She ran her hand through her hair, pushing it back from her face as she blew out her breath.

"Well, I'll let you go. Make your phone calls," Jodie said. "Let me know how this all works out."

"I will."

Lauren ended the phone call, looking at the unfinished arrangement sitting in front of her, the implications of what Vic had just done slowly settling into her soul.

He had found the document he knew existed.

And once he found it, he'd given up the rights laid out in it.

Why would he do that?

Had Dean changed his mind about ranching? She pushed herself away from her stool and walked to the front of the store, where her aunt was just handing Jane Forsythe her receipt.

"Hey, there, Lauren," Jane said, smiling, as Lauren stopped by her aunt. "How are you doing?"

"I'm good. I understand Vic Moore was at the office today?"

"Yeah. He just left half an hour ago."

"Did he say where he was going after that?"

"I imagine back to the ranch. He said something about having to work with one of his horses."

"Thanks." Lauren couldn't call him, because his number was plugged into her phone, which was sitting on her desk at the ranch. She turned to her aunt, touching her shoulder. "I need to go" was all she said.

"Of course. Thanks for coming."

Lauren gave her a quick hug. "Thanks for your help."

"Where are you going?"

"I'm going to talk to Vic."

The colt turned away from Vic and once again he waved his rope at it and sent it around the round pen in the arena, the dust from its hooves settling in the warm summer air trapped in the building.

Stubborn horse simply wouldn't give.

When Vic had come back from town, he'd needed to keep busy doing something. Anything. He hadn't talked to Dean yet, explained to him what had happened and what he had done.

Working with this colt was a way of putting that conversation off.

A couple of times he'd felt a chill of regret

at what he'd done, but each time he did, he thought of what Lauren had told him.

How she'd given up everything for everybody. He heard the pain in her voice. Sensed the depth of the sacrifices she had made.

Keith had often mentioned how frustrated he was with his daughters. But when Vic sat and talked with Drake today, after making his decision to rip up the lease agreement, he'd found out more about Keith's expectations of young girls whom he'd barely known and barely gotten to know.

He, who had grown up with loving parents and a caring community, couldn't imagine the loneliness and responsibility that must have haunted Lauren.

The colt whinnied at him, lowering its head, tonguing its mouth.

He stopped and let the colt come toward him, waiting for its response, ready to reward it.

"It's okay," he said, his voice steady, even, while his thoughts spun and doubled back in his head.

Why had he done what he had? What would happen to Dean? Why had he ruined their one big chance?

He stilled the noisy voices in his head as he reached out and gently touched the colt's withers. It flinched and he drew back, but then the colt came close again.

"It will be all right," he told the colt, gently stroking its side, rewarding the movement toward him.

Please, Lord, let that be so.

And as he prayed, the noisy, accusing voices grew still.

He heard the creak of a door and he half turned, expecting to see Dean come storming in to accuse him of ruining his future in yet another way.

But the blond hair and lithe figure belonged to someone else. Someone who had been on his mind since the first time he had seen her sitting in Drake's office.

She stood silhouetted against the light dancing through her hair, casting her features in shadow.

He couldn't read her expression.

So he waited for her to come closer. To make the first move.

Just like the colt he'd been working with.

She stood there, then, slowly, she started walking toward him.

He waited until she came to the metal door of the round pen, then joined her.

She stood in front of him, looking bemused.

"I talked to Jodie about what you did," she said. Her voice was quiet. "I can't believe… I don't know…" She stopped there, her voice fading away, and then, to his shock and surprise, he saw her eyes well up.

He'd thought he would be able to keep his cool. Keep his distance.

But the silent slide of tears down her cheek melted his already shaky resolve.

He closed the gap between them in two steps, took her in his arms and drew her close to him. Her arms slipped around him, her head tucking under his chin.

They stood there, the moment lengthening, words unnecessary.

Vic stroked her hair, absorbing the fact that she was here. She had come to him.

Finally she drew back and wiped her cheeks, releasing a self-conscious laugh. "Sorry."

"Nothing to apologize for," he said, smoothing away a few tears from her cheek.

She looked up at him, a question in her eyes.

"Why didn't you follow through? With the lease agreement. Why did you rip it up?"

"That sounds dramatic," he said. "I just got Drake to run it through the shredder."

She gave him a tentative smile. "Why did

you let him do that? It was what you've been looking for ever since I got here."

He paused, giving himself time to choose the right words.

"I did it because I wanted you to be able to do what you wanted. I did it for you."

She slowly shook her head, as if trying to figure out what he was saying. What he had done.

He had to tell her. Now he really had nothing to lose by her knowing.

"I did it because I love you," he finally said. "I wanted you to be able to decide your own future and take your own path."

Lauren's eyes grew wide; her lips parted as astonishment crept over her features.

"You love me?"

"I do. I love you."

She grabbed the back of his neck, pulled his head down and kissed him, her fingers tangling in his hair, her other arm clinging to him.

His first reaction was surprise, his second a shivering warmth.

He pulled her closer. Finally they drew back.

"I can't believe this," she whispered, her hands stroking his face, her fingers trailing over his features. "I can't believe you would do this for me. No one has ever done anything like that."

"Like I said, I did it because I love you. I had no expectations."

"I know you didn't." She rested her hands on his shoulders. "But it meant so much to me. It showed me something deep within me that took some time for me to acknowledge."

"Which is?" he gently prompted.

She looked up at him again, a warm smile curving her lips. "That you are the best person I've ever met. That you are a wonderful, caring man. That I know I can trust you with my life. With my heart." She stood up on tiptoe and brushed a welcome kiss over his lips. "I love you, too, Vic Moore."

Her words created a rush of joy in his heart.

"I'm glad. Makes it easier to talk about a future."

"We have a future?" she asked, her smile turning adorably coy.

"I want a future. With you. I want you by my side and I want to be by your side."

"I want the same," she said.

He kissed her again, sealing their promises. But as he drew away, another reality intruded.

"And what about your business?" he asked. "Your partnership with Amy."

"I've done more phoning the last hour than I've done since I got here," Lauren said, curling her hands behind his neck, leaning back to hold his gaze. "I wanted everything decided before I came here to you. I told Alex the ranch wasn't for sale, but I directed him to Amy. Put them in touch. I talked to Amy on the way here and I believe they are setting something up. She's disappointed I won't be working with her. We are good friends and have always gotten along well."

"That won't change," Vic assured her.

"I don't think so. I think Alex is willing to invest in the company and let her direct how things will be run."

"So once again you've taken care of the other people in your life," he said in a teasing tone.

"It's what I do." She gave him another smile. "And you shouldn't complain, because I hope to do the same for you."

"That doesn't make you very independent," he said. "I know that was important to you."

"I think I have a solution. I wouldn't be surprised if Aunt Laura would be willing to let me take over her flower shop. Maybe sooner than later."

"Would you be okay with that?"

Lauren nodded, her expression growing softer. "I think I would like it more than running an accounting business."

"You look happy just thinking about it," he said, another concern fading away.

"I've always loved helping her."

"And you love flowers and plants."

"Not as much as I love you," she said.

Vic kissed her again and then felt a nudge behind him. He turned to see the colt he'd been working with, head hanging over the gate, trying to get his attention.

"Looks like someone's ready to work with me," Vic said, half turning to touch the colt's head. Acknowledge its presence.

"Some things just take time," Lauren said, touching the colt herself. "It's a matter of trust, I think."

Vic grew serious and turned back to Lauren. "I know you've been burned in the past. But I want you to know that you can trust me."

Lauren gave him a warm smile, then kissed him again. "I know that, and I do. I trust you with my heart and my life."

"I won't let you down." He slipped his arm over her shoulder, pulling her close. "And now I suppose we'll have to go talk to our family. Let them know what's happening."

Lauren's smile grew even broader. "Our family. I sure like the sound of that."

"So do I."

And together they walked out of the barn and into their future.

* * * * *

If you loved this story, pick up the first
BIG SKY COWBOYS *book,*
WRANGLING THE COWBOY'S HEART
and these other stories of love in Montana
from bestselling author
Carolyne Aarsen:

HER COWBOY HERO
REUNITED WITH THE COWBOY
THE COWBOY'S HOMECOMING

Available now from Love Inspired!
Find more great reads at
www.LoveInspired.com

Dear Reader,

Lauren's experiences dealt her hard lessons in trust. As a result she tried to find her own way through life, thinking that owning her own business and being independent will give her what she needs. But though she had a good plan, she needed to find a way to blend her heart's desire with a life's plan. I hope you enjoyed reading Lauren and Vic's story.

I love to hear from readers. If you want to write me, you can contact me at caarsen@xplornet.com. As well, if you want to find out more about other books in the series or other books I have written, check out my website at www.carolyneaarsen.com. While you're there, sign up for my newsletter to be kept up-to-date on any new books I have coming out and just general news from our place.

Carolyne Aarsen

LARGER-PRINT BOOKS!

GET 2 FREE
LARGER-PRINT NOVELS
PLUS 2 FREE
MYSTERY GIFTS

Love Inspired®

SUSPENSE

RIVETING INSPIRATIONAL ROMANCE

Larger-print novels are now available...

REQUEST YOUR FREE BOOKS!
2 FREE WHOLESOME ROMANCE NOVELS IN LARGER PRINT
PLUS 2
FREE
MYSTERY GIFTS

ᴗ ᴗ ᴗ ᴗ ᴗ ᴗ ᴗ ᴗ ᴗ ᴗ ᴗ ᴗ ᴗ ᴗ ᴗ ᴗ ᴗ ᴗ ᴗ ᴗ

HEARTWARMING™

❊❊❊❊❊❊❊❊❊❊❊❊❊❊❊❊❊❊❊❊❊❊

Wholesome, tender romances

YES! Please send me 2 FREE Harlequin® Heartwarming Larger-Print novels and my 2 FREE mystery gifts (gifts worth about $10). After receiving them, if I don't wish to receive any more books, I can return the shipping statement marked "cancel." If I don't cancel, I will receive 4 brand-new larger-print novels every month and be billed just $5.24 per book in the U.S. or $5.99 per book in Canada. That's a savings of at least 19% off the cover price. It's quite a bargain! Shipping and handling is just 50¢ per book in the U.S. and 75¢ per book in Canada.* I understand that accepting the 2 free books and gifts places me under no obligation to buy anything. I can always return a shipment and cancel at any time. Even if I never buy another book, the two free books and gifts are mine to keep forever.

161/361 IDN GHX2

Name	(PLEASE PRINT)	
Address		Apt. #
City	State/Prov.	Zip/Postal Code

Signature (if under 18, a parent or guardian must sign)

Mail to the **Reader Service:**
IN U.S.A.: P.O. Box 1867, Buffalo, NY 14240-1867
IN CANADA: P.O. Box 609, Fort Erie, Ontario L2A 5X3

* Terms and prices subject to change without notice. Prices do not include applicable taxes. Sales tax applicable in N.Y. Canadian residents will be charged applicable taxes. Offer not valid in Quebec. This offer is limited to one order per household. Not valid for current subscribers to Harlequin Heartwarming larger-print books. All orders subject to credit approval. Credit or debit balances in a customer's account(s) may be offset by any other outstanding balance owed by or to the customer. Please allow 4 to 6 weeks for delivery. Offer available while quantities last.

HWI5

WESTERN WP PROMISES

YES! Please send me **The Western Promises Collection** in Larger Print. This collection begins with 3 FREE books and 2 FREE gifts (gifts valued at approx. $14.00 retail) in the first shipment, along with the other first 4 books from the collection! If I do not cancel, I will receive 8 monthly shipments until I have the entire 51-book Western Promises collection. I will receive 2 or 3 FREE books in each shipment and I will pay just $4.99 US/ $5.89 CDN for each of the other four books in each shipment, plus $2.99 for shipping and handling per shipment. *If I decide to keep the entire collection, I'll have paid for only 32 books, because 19 books are FREE! I understand that accepting the 3 free books and gifts places me under no obligation to buy anything. I can always return a shipment and cancel at any time. My free books and gifts are mine to keep no matter what I decide.

272 HCN 3070 472 HCN 3070

Name _____ (PLEASE PRINT) _____

Address _____ Apt. # _____

City _____ State/Prov. _____ Zip/Postal Code _____

Signature (if under 18, a parent or guardian must sign)

Mail to the **Reader Service:**
IN U.S.A.: P.O. Box 1867, Buffalo, NY 14240-1867
IN CANADA: P.O. Box 609, Fort Erie, Ontario L2A 5X3

* Terms and prices subject to change without notice. Prices do not include applicable taxes. Sales tax applicable in N.Y. Canadian residents will be charged applicable taxes. This offer is limited to one order per household. All orders subject to approval. Credit or debit balances in a customer's account(s) may be offset by any other outstanding balance owed by or to the customer. Please allow 4 to 6 weeks for delivery. Offer available while quantities last. Offer not available to Quebec residents.